HOUSE OF GAMES

Belle Fleur Erotica Volume 2

Nicolas Blanc

Minuet Publishing[2]

---

1. https://minuetpublishing.wixsite.com/books

2. https://minuetpublishing.wixsite.com/books

Zoe is determined to be the sole focus of Martin's attention, but
Martin has a long-time lover, Elke, who comes in and out of their lives
as she pleases.
Zoe gives Martin an ultimatum to choose between the two women,
and Martin gives her a game.
Elke will give Martin and Zoe a sexual challenge, and if they succeed,
they win that round. Martin will then give Elke a challenge.
The first to fail a challenge loses the game.
If Elke loses, then she is out of Martin's life.
If Zoe loses, then she must submit to Elke and leave Martin and Paris.
Each erotic challenge gets more dangerous and perverted.
Who will win in the House of Games?

'Love is like a tree: it grows by itself, roots itself deeply in our being and continues to flourish over a heart in ruin. The inexplicable fact is that the blinder it is, the more tenacious it is. It is never stronger than when it is completely unreasonable.'
Victor Hugo, *The Hunchback of Notre-Dame*

3

WET

From her college dormitory bedroom window, Zoe Fabrice observed a bustling scene of students and academics scurrying to class. The cobblestone pathways, adorned with ivy-covered stone walls, were bathed in the gentle warmth of the morning sun. From the rooftop of the building on the opposite side of the quadrangle courtyard, carved stone gargoyles, like her, gazed down from above.

The vacation period spent working for Mr. Dore felt surreal, like a fleeting dream. She had traded the twisted sexual adventures of that time for quiet times in the library, flirtatious conversations with her professor, and a burgeoning relationship with Leon. He was an attentive lover, always caressing her gently and whispering sweet words in her ear. Nonetheless, she felt a void that needed to be filled. She chose not to reveal the details of her time working for Mr. Dore or the disturbing fantasies that plagued her during her private moments.

'Don't turn around.'

The voice sent shivers down her spine with its gravelly and dark timbre. The sound of Mr. Dore's voice came out of nowhere, catching her off guard. Three months had passed since she last heard that voice.

'Unzip your skirt,' Mr Dore commanded.

Zoe took a deep breath in.

'Do it now,' Mr Dore said with a harshness she had not heard before.

Zoe replied nervously, 'Yes, sir,' as she unzipped her skirt at the side and allowed it to fall to the floor, leaving nothing but her white cotton panties covering her behind.

'Where have you been, Mr Dore?' Zoe asked. 'I was so worried about you.'

'I ask the questions, Zoe. Never forget that.'

'I'm sorry, sir.'

'Now unhook your bra and let it fall to the floor as well. Lean forward against the window with your legs apart.'

Zoe paused for a long time, then said, 'Yes, sir.'

As Mr Dore's hands explored Zoe's body, she could feel the warmth of his touch on her bare skin and the sensation of her nipples becoming sensitive and protruding through her soft T-shirt. He smelt rich and musky.

Zoe started to turn, but Mr Dore then said, 'Don't look at me and lift your bottom higher.'

Zoe thought that Mr. Dore's voice had become noticeably harsher, and his words had an edge to them. To her surprise, she found herself irresistibly drawn to him, her heart beating faster than ever. She could feel the hunger pulsating through her, making her body ache. She wondered what experiences had shaped him during their months apart.

With a wider stance, Zoe arched her back, raising her backside. She then felt Mr Dore's hand flat against her buttock.

'Who does this belong to?'

'You, sir.'

'Now lift your feet up so you are standing on the tips of your toes.'

'Yes, sir.'

Zoe then felt the firm touch of Mr. Dore's hand running up and down one leg and then the other. He then gently caressed her inner thighs with two fingers, moving in a slow, rhythmic motion until her legs trembled.

'Stay on your toes, Zoe. Don't disappoint me. I have been thinking of you for so long.'

'Yes, sir.'

'I have missed you.'

'I have missed you too, sir.'

'I can tell,' said Mr Dore, feeling the wetness between Zoe's legs and seeing the damp circle at the crotch of her panties.

'Are you ready to work for me again, Zoe?'

'Yes, sir.'

'Now stand up straight and with your legs straight, roll your panties down your legs and hand them to me but don't turn around,' said Mr Dore, his tone somewhat affectionate but firm.

Zoe followed the instructions carefully, feeling the cool air against her bare skin as she slid her panties down her legs. She waved the panties behind her, waiting for Mr Dore to take them from her. However, instead of taking them from her, he stood there silently, his eyes fixed on her, examining her every move as she waved them behind her.

'Place your panties in your mouth,' said Mr Dore.

'Yes, sir,' said Zoe, before rolling the cotton panties into a tight ball and placing them in her mouth. Her jaw stretched out to take the full ball of them.'

Zoe wondered whether anyone on campus could see her standing there. Her nipples poking through her T-shirt and her panties rolled up in a ball in her mouth.

'Now Zoe, imagine you are a fine racehorse and wag your tail for me,' said Mr Dore, polite now but firm.

Zoe swayed her behind one way and then the other.

'Very good. Zoe.'

'Now imagine that your hand is the racehorse, and you are the jockey. Place your fingers as far into you as they will go,' said Mr Dore.

'Now ride those fingers like you are riding a horse,' Mr Dore said.

Zoe moved up and down upon her fingers like they were a horse that she was riding. Moving herself up and down upon them.'

Then Zoe heard a whoosh and felt the crack of a riding crop against both cheeks of her buttocks. She involuntarily winced in pain.

'Giddy up, Zoe,' said Mr Dore as Zoe recovered her composure and then continued to ride her fingers, her bottom still smarting from the riding crop. Her legs trembled at the thought of being struck again.

'You have reached the home straight. Ride that pony for all she is worth. Ride hard, Zoe, and I will not need to use the riding crop again.'

Zoe bounced upon her fingers with intensity, her breath panting. She felt the riding crop trailing up and down her bare buttocks. She then heard the swoosh of the riding crop through the air and froze for impact, but it did not come.

'Did I tell you to stop, Zoe?' There was almost a cruel snigger to Mr Dore's voice.

'No, sir,' gasped Zoe, her fingers of her left hand still halfway within her. With all the energy she could muster, she started riding them again.

'You are the most talented jockey in town, mounted on your saddle, your feet in the stirrups and the wind whipping past you. The crowd is cheering you,' Mr Dore said as Zoe started to pant. 'Can you hear them, Zoe?'

'Yes...sir,' said Zoe breathlessly.

'Ride that pony harder,' Mr Dore commanded.

'Yes, ah, sir,' Zoe said, the delicious pressure building up to an almost unbearable point.

'Now Zoe stop.'

Zoe did not want to stop. She was so close to climaxing, but she knew she had to obey Mr Dore.

'Now show me. Part your lips for me so I can see,' said Mr Dore.

Zoe's voice trembled slightly as she said, 'Yes, sir,' and she slowly spread her legs, revealing the most private part of herself to Mr Dore that was pulsing like a beating heart.

'Are you wet, Zoe?'

'Yes, sir.'

'Who are you wet for?'

'You, sir.'

Zoe then felt a finger delicately tracing a path downwards between her legs. The overwhelming sensation pushed her to the breaking point.

As her fuse was blown, she experienced a mix of overwhelming sensations and a strange sense of detachment. As she released control, a wave of euphoria consumed her completely. It felt as if tiny, electric shocks were pulsating in all directions beneath her skin. She could feel the tension coursing through her body, making it difficult for her to stay upright.

It was then that Zoe noticed a soft exhale from someone else in the room. It sounded like a man. She started to turn her head, curious to see who it was, but Mr. Dore's forceful command made her freeze. 'I said, don't turn around.'

'But who's that with you?' asked Zoe.

'Remember,' Mr Dore said sternly, 'I'm the one asking the questions.'

WAITING

Zoe Fabrice reclined on Raymond Garnier's desk. Her body exuded an irresistible allure. Her appearance was a mesmerizing blend of elegance and sensuality, surpassing even the Venus De Milo. The candlelight cast a warm glow on her, emphasizing her soft curves and flawless skin.

Zoe, far from being a statue, was an untamed beast, her breath ragged as her fingers explored the territory between her thighs. As she stroked herself, a wave of electrifying sensations coursed through her body, transporting her to a realm beyond rationality.

It was undeniable that Zoe was a masterpiece in every sense. Her stockings, with their two black seams, accentuated the contours of her well-defined calves and shapely legs, leading the eye to the black garters and stocking tops that framed the muscle divots of her thighs. Resting above the black fishnet stockings was a perky derriere, seemingly asking for a playful slap.

Zoe had the reputation of being one of the most beautiful women in Paris. Her womanly curves were admired both on the catwalk and in the halls of her university. Since meeting Martin, she liked to dress to provoke a reaction rather than like the shy young woman she really was. Zoe now liked tight fitting plaid skirts that hugged her curves and richly patterned stockings that immediately caught the eye.

All the students and professors turned to watch her as she passed. She had the kind of beauty that once seen could not be forgotten, her image playing in the back of your mind like a beautiful dream.

Notwithstanding her obvious beauty, Zoe still sometimes felt insecure about her body, worrying that her breasts weren't large enough and that her body was too thin. Martin reassured her, giving her constant compliments, making her feel so good. Yet he set challenges for her like this.

Martin liked to keep her on edge. He was terrified of a life of suburban domesticity and wanted them both to live on that knife edge instead. Here in Raymond's small study Zoe feels pleasure and warmth throughout her body and yet she still feels a terrible sense of foreboding that makes the sensations of pleasure tinged with a feeling of being unmoored from reality like she is no longer a normal Parisian girl, but a wild thing unmoored from morality.

Ever since Martin Dore reentered her life, she had abandoned her reserved and shy nature, embracing her untamed and audacious side. Five minutes earlier that evening she was a normal girl seated around a table enjoying a dinner party with her boyfriend, Martin Dore, Martin's friend, Raymond and his wife, and other guests, drinking wine, making polite small talk, and laughing at their jokes in a very handsome and comfortable middle-class home in central Paris. She could now feel the intense pleasure building within her, but Mr. Dore's instructions forbade her from reaching climax.

Outside, the wind howled like the turmoil Zoe felt inside. Her eyes were covered by a black velvet blindfold that she had applied to herself, wrapped around her brunette ringlets. She had lit two candles as instructed and placed them on the desk. Her bare breasts were rubbing against the mahogany wood. Her nipples brushed the surface of the wood. Zoe's black bra and shiny crimson cocktail dress were down below her breasts. Her long legs stretched out sinuously in black silk stockings. She wore high shiny black Manolo Blahnik heels which stretched her calves and caused a delicate lilt to her bottom. Zoe's legs seemed incredibly long in those shoes. The night black satin shoes with a crystal jewel buckle were like the baroque frame around Madame Pompadour at The Louvre, a frame for a great work of art.

Zoe could hear the dinner party downstairs. Raymond, the host, was telling a joke. There was a titter of laughter, then the clink of glasses before the guests took a large mouthful of red wine. Zoe wondered for a moment what she was doing there in the study. It all seemed incredibly silly for a moment - her, the young introvert wantonly displaying herself in the older man's study. Why? It was all because of

Martin's damned game. A very dangerous game that Zoe struggled to understand the rules of. All she knew was that she had to get through this contest and prevail if she wanted Martin to herself. Following Martin's instructions, Zoe's black panties were discreetly placed in the drawer of Raymond's desk. With her right hand, she held up the back of her red satin cocktail dress, while her left hand found comfort between her legs.

The sensation from her fingers was already bringing her close to orgasm. She could feel that her breasts were fuller. Her nipples were hard little nubs. Zoe's heart pounded. Her breath was quick, and her fingers were slick. She felt red hot embarrassment mixed with beautiful tension. She had to not climax. Not yet. She had to resist no matter how tempting it was. She had to not let herself tip over the edge. To do so would mean that she would fail this challenge. Raymond had to empty his seed within her first. She had to drain him before she could orgasm. Everything rested on winning this damned game.

If she was not aroused, Raymond would notice that. If she had already reached orgasm, Raymond would notice that too. Raymond was Martin's business partner and was very detail oriented. He always brought Martin back after he had embarked on some wild business idea. Raymond noticed everything. It was his way of feeling in control of a chaotic universe.

Zoe could feel herself teetering then, flushed with both warmth and weightlessness. She could almost not stand another second. She was about to tip over the edge when she heard someone coming up the stairs and then turning the door handle. Zoe froze.

The sound of the dinner party was suddenly louder as the door opened. She could almost feel Raymond's gaze, peering into the barely illuminated study and could almost hear his jaw drop seeing her there, her bare bottom shining in the red candlelight. Raymond blinked and tried to catch his breath.

'Zoe, I'm so sorry. I didn't know you were in here,' said Raymond, shocked and standing there, looking like a college professor in houndstooth and tweed, who had come across a naughty college student masturbating on his desk.

'Oh my,' Zoe said softly, her voice a mix of shyness and seduction, as she turned her blindfolded head and discreetly covered her damp crotch with her hand. It captivated Raymond's attention even more. He could see how her cheeks flushed and her breathing quickened, revealing her arousal. She was practically pulsating with anticipation.

Zoe vividly recalled the instruction, her mind replaying the words like a broken record. Raymond's heart raced as he witnessed her vulnerability, her body trembling with ecstasy, and a sense of excitement washed over him.

'I should have knocked. So sorry,' said Raymond, sounding flustered.

'I'm so embarrassed. I'm the one who should apologize,' said Zoe. 'I was looking for the bathroom and came across your study.'

'Don't be embarrassed,' said Raymond.

'But I am,' said Zoe in a meek voice.

Raymond tried to collect his thoughts then said, 'You know it's charming to see you like this. I've had a crush on you for as long as I can remember.'

'I've been lusting after you too,' said Zoe.

'Why were you wearing a blindfold?'

'It was part of my fantasy.'

Zoe removed the hand covering herself and stroked again, the warm feeling spread through her again. She turned and smiled at Raymond. He couldn't help but stare at her small tender core, the delicate pink cleft with wide open lips, wet and exposed. Her thighs were spread out as far as they could go.

Raymond looked Zoe up and down. Her skin blushed crimson like she had been too close to a fire. The redness of her skin in the candlelight just made her seem even more beautiful to him. Zoe's hair fell around the blindfold. Below the black material, her ruby red lips were parted, revealing bright white teeth.

Raymond imagined for a moment kissing that perfect red mouth. Before he did not even dream, there was any chemistry between them. He just thought she was being polite, laughing at his dirty jokes. He did not in his wildest dreams imagine she was so into him.

Raymond had been totally charmed by Zoe for such a long time. All night he had been staring at her beautiful face, long legs, and graceful manner. Raymond had been so jealous of Martin and often thought about being with Zoe but never dreamed it would happen. Looking at her now, she was even more magical than in his fantasies. He felt himself getting hot and swollen.

'It's just I have this fantasy,' said Zoe, allowing her red cocktail dress to fall to cover her behind.

'Yes.'

'Of you taking me on your desk,' said Zoe.

She couldn't believe the words coming out of her mouth.

Raymond's stunned gaze was fixed on her as he whispered, 'I'm honored but...my wife is downstairs with Martin and Cary and Evangeline.'

Zoe, whispering back, reassured him, 'It's just a fantasy. It can just stay as a fantasy. You won't tell anyone, will you?'

Raymond, confused, asked, 'About what?'

Zoe shyly looked up at him, her bright red lips forming a smile.

Raymond took a step forward, unable to resist the magnetic pull of Zoe's arousal. In a trance-like state, he moved closer to her. Suddenly, Raymond's wife, Charlotte, called out his name from the dining table, interrupting their moment.

Raymond quickly came up with an excuse, 'Just looking for my bottle of Pierre Brevin. I'll be down in a minute.'

As he closed the study door behind him, Raymond quietly instructed Zoe, 'Turn around, Zoe. Show me what happens in your fantasy.'

Downstairs, laughter echoed through the house. Zoe complied, facing the desk once again and slowly raising her cocktail dress to reveal the black fishnet stockings fastened with black suspender belts adorned with gold sliders.

She lifted her dress even higher, exposing her bare behind and the space between her legs. Each stocking had a satin bow at the back.

Intrigued, Raymond asked, 'Where are your panties?'

Zoe confidently replied, 'In your desk drawer.'

The sound of Raymond lighting a cigarette filled the air as he took in the scene before him.

'This is really something,' he sighed.

Zoe purred, 'You are really something. I'm fascinated by older men.'

'You are truly the most beautiful young woman I have ever seen,' said Raymond, examining Zoe's exquisite curves.

'This is my birthday gift to you,' said Zoe breathlessly. 'I want to do anything that will make you happy.'

'I'm flattered, Zoe, but Charlotte is probably downstairs now serving dessert.'

Zoe hiked her dress up further and moved her legs apart then says, 'I'm your dessert.'

'Zoe, this is crazy.'

Not assisting me in achieving my fantasy would be crazy. Ray, life is short. I need you now. I'm soaked,' Zoe said, as her fingers played along the inside of her thighs.

Raymond couldn't help but admire Zoe's stunning, long brunette hair cascading down her back and perfectly wrapped with the blindfold. He longed to run his fingers through that silky hair. Zoe's lips were pressed together, her face flushed with desire and shame, as droplets dripped onto the wooden floor.

'Ray, please,' Zoe pleaded, her fingers dancing along the rim, their touch conveying her longing.

Zoe thought about the instructions she had been given. She had to do exactly what Martin has told her. She stopped stroking for a moment and there was silence in the room. There was no sound but the clink of glasses and laughing from the dining room downstairs.

'Don't stop, Zoe,' croaked Raymond as he walked towards her. He stroked her hair with one hand while drawing upon the cigarette with the other.

Zoe continued to stimulate herself. Raymond felt boundless passion for this beautiful young woman. In that moment, nothing else held any significance. His heart thumped loudly in his ears, drowning out all the other sounds. He desperately wanted to take her, his heart pounding with desire. He wanted to consume her completely, his body pressed against hers. As he touched her, he marveled at the contrast between her softness and his hardness. He yearned to surrender himself entirely to her, to be enveloped by her essence. To disappear into her. To fly away with her to some place beautiful and free.

Raymond then heard his wife's voice downstairs again, and this brought him back to reality for a moment.

'Have you found the wine?'

'Not yet.'

'You have found me,' said Zoe quietly.

'I don't think if I just stroke your hair that would count as infidelity,' said Raymond, as he sat in the desk chair and looked at Zoe.

'I need you so badly,' whispered Zoe.

Raymond touched Zoe's face like she was something magical. She had a delicate perfume of lilac and roses.

'Slow your caressing down. Just do it slowly now. Allow the sensations just to permeate you,' said Raymond in a harsh whisper.

'Yes, sir,' said Zoe.

'I remember you when you first started working for Martin. You were beautiful then, but you are even more beautiful now.'

Zoe closed her eyes, shutting out the world around her. At that point, she was drenched, and her skin felt as salty as a mermaid's. She was at the end of her rope and could feel her grip slipping away. She knew that she must not climax until Ray did, but all he seemed interested in was gently stroking her hair.

'My fantasy involves you kissing me,' said Zoe breathlessly.

Raymond stood just inches away from her, his breath warm on her neck. Raymond extinguished the cigarette, its smoke lingering in the air, and studied the look of pure delight on Zoe's face. How could he not have felt Zoe's desire for him before? Raymond leaned forward and kissed Zoe's soft lips while his hand glanced along the curve of her breast.

'Your lips are so soft, and you smell so handsome,' said Zoe. 'Now you caress me between my legs.'

Raymond moved silently behind Zoe, his gaze fixated on her fingers as they caressed the sensitive area between her thighs. He leaned in, studying her features with a discerning eye. Her lips had become swollen and had a soft, inviting appearance.

'Please touch me, Raymond. I need your touch so badly,' said Zoe.

Raymond inched forward, his heart pounding in his chest. His hot breath sent shivers down Zoe's spine as it caressed the back of her neck. He gently lifted her hair and planted a soft kiss on the back of her neck, causing a delightful tingle to travel down Zoe's spine.

'Zoe, you're so wet. Is all this really for me?'

'I want to taste my arousal,' whispers Zoe.

Raymond rubs the silky wetness between his fingers. Zoe smiles and nods, waiting for him, every sense tingling with anticipation.

'Open your mouth,' says Raymond.

'Yes, sir.'

Raymond's gaze fixated on Zoe, who licked her lips with anticipation before forming a perfect O with her pursed lips to receive his fingers. Raymond slipped two fingers into her mouth, and Zoe savored the taste of her honey sweetness, eliciting a soft moan. Zoe's hands explored the intimate space between her legs, indulging in her own sensations as she sensually sucked on Ray's fingers.

'Spank me,' said Zoe.

'What?'

'Spank me for being a naughty girl and dripping on your nice, clean study floor.'

Raymond was dumb struck staring at her while Zoe positively panted in anticipation.

Ray moved his hand up and then lightly onto Zoe's buttock.

'That's not how you do it,' said Zoe, spanking her own buttock hard enough to cause a slight red handprint.

'They'll hear us downstairs,' said Raymond in a panic now.

'Tell them I was a bad girl,' whispered Zoe as she teased her clitoris with her fingers, just removing her fingers in time to avoid climaxing.

'It doesn't seem right,' said Raymond.

'Something that feels so right can't be wrong,' sighed Zoe.

'I don't know.'

'Please Ray - spank me now. Hard. Make me squeal. I can't wait any longer.'

Raymond raised his hand and let it crash onto Zoe's buttock, the sound echoing through the empty room. As he paused, the sound of joyful chatter and laughter from his guests reached his ears. He imagined Charlotte captivating the guests with her usual animated storytelling, the room hanging on her every word. He let out a sigh of relief, grateful that his wife was spared from hearing the resounding slap. Zoe certainly felt it. Her soft round derriere has a prominent red handprint on it.

'Ray, I'll show you what I want you to do with your cock,' says Zoe, sliding her fingers into herself from behind, pumping them in and out of herself. 'Spank me again. Hard.'

Raymond playfully spanked Zoe's other buttock, adding a jolt of sensation to her already intense pleasure.

'I need you so badly, Ray,' said Zoe. 'I really can't wait any longer.'

Zoe then sensually rubbed herself up and down the corner of Raymond's desk, savoring the friction against her body.

'I need you right now,' panted Zoe. 'Spank me again.'

With each spank, Ray propelled Zoe towards the brink, her body pressed against the desk's rough surface. With a powerful thrust, he penetrated Zoe from behind, eliciting a deep sigh of pleasure. She embraced him tightly, her warmth radiating against his skin, and let out a low, sensuous moan.

'Grab me by my hips and drive into me while you spank me,' said Zoe. 'Drive me all the way home.'

With unbridled enthusiasm, Raymond followed Zoe's every command, his eyes welling up with tears of ecstasy as he intimately pressed himself against Zoe, aligning their bodies, his heated breath mingling with hers, as he experienced the sensation of being engulfed by her, pulled into her depths like a swirling whirlpool.

Zoe's desire for him soaked through every inch of her being. His thrusting motion sent waves of pleasure cascading through her, starting from her most intimate place and radiating outwards, igniting every nerve ending. Through Raymond's rhythmic pressure, the forces of nature converged within them, resulting in a floating sensation and a feeling of warmth.

Zoe felt his firm presence against her backside. The force of each thrust pressed her firmly against the desk. With a soft touch, he caressed each of Zoe's breasts, his fingers tracing delicate patterns on her skin. It felt like electricity was running through her body. She felt her heartbeat pulse in her center as her spine tingled. He quivered, succumbing to the sensation of her, and exploded deep within her. She too is helpless against the tempest of pleasure and finally surrendered to all its terrible beauty until they were both spent, warm, and silent as they breathed heavily as one being.

GUESTS

All the guests at the dinner party could clearly see that Charlotte had put in a lot of effort. She had prepared a mouthwatering feast, featuring multiple courses of delectable dishes made with fresh ingredients from the market. The aroma filled the room. Charlotte had also gone to great lengths to dress for the evening, wearing a strappy glitzy sheer mini dress with a plunging neckline. When choosing the dress, she had been determined not to be outshone by Zoe, Martin's girlfriend and former maid. She handpicked a dress that accentuated her figure and exuded elegance. She looked around, wondering where Raymond could be. He has been gone now for a good ten minutes. Whenever she needed him, Raymond seemed to evaporate into thin air. And where is Zoe?

Charlotte's heart had always belonged to Raymond ever since she first laid eyes on him at Lycée Saint Louis de Gonzague. However, she couldn't help but be captivated by Martin Dore, Raymond's business partner, and his stunning girlfriend, Zoe Fabrice. She was well-acquainted with all the whispered conversations and hidden truths. She knew that Zoe, who used to work for him, had become a student at Université PSL. Besides her big eyes and sexy smile, she had also made a name for herself as a model, appearing in Vogue, L'Officiel, and Madame Figaro. Having such an attractive girlfriend only heightened Martin's appeal. Charlotte's mind wandered as she imagined Martin's prowess in the bedroom.

Martin always had an air of intrigue surrounding him. She had always enjoyed his company, but she yearned to unravel the mystery hidden beneath his charming smile and captivating, noble eyes. She could see Cary and Evangeline laughing and chatting with him, clearly enjoying his company. Martin's hair had a touch of grey now, making him look older than the last time she saw him. His chin, usually clean-cut, now bore a rugged and snowy appearance.

'Some people said philosophy teaches us nothing. I say it taught us everything,' said Martin, taking a sip of red wine.

'How so?' said Evangeline.

'Just think about Camus's famous saying - joy is an act of defiance. There was so much we could learn from that. Or what about Marcus Aurelius saying life is tough but you can be tougher. Or Sartre - you always have a choice.'

'What did you get if you crossed a philosopher with a godfather? An offer you couldn't understand,' joked Cary.

'Philosophers mined the rich vein of experience. You hadn't really lived if you had not been a philosopher,' said Martin.

'But which philosophers really lived their philosophy?' asked Evangeline.

'Georges Bataille drenched his life in erotic hedonism and transgression. He said, 'Beauty is desired in order that it may be befouled; not for its own sake, but for the joy brought by the certainty of profaning it." said Martin.

'What did that mean?' asked Charlotte, placing a slice of apple cranberry galette in front of Martin.

'You tell me,' smiled Martin.

'We derived pleasure in corrupting beauty?' said Evangeline.

'Wasn't that what we were put on the planet to do?' laughed Cary.

Charlotte returned to the kitchen, then placed a plate in front of the empty chairs of Raymond and Charlotte.

'We derived pleasure in transgression such as taking something beautiful and making it profane,' said Martin. 'Transgression was a wild energy. We wanted what was forbidden. Think of the joy that Madonna expressed in dancing in the music video for Like a Prayer. Madonna took Christian imagery and used it for a song about romantic transcendence.'

'Who would have thought that stigmata and crosses could be so sexy?' said Cary.

'Madonna harnessed the power of transgression, and she became one of the most popular pop culture figures of all time,' said Martin.

'Not all of us could be Madonna,' said Evangeline.

'Why not?' asked Martin.

'A pointy bra would not suit me,' laughed Cary.

'I didn't know,' said Evangeline. 'You could express your feminine side.'

'Hey, why couldn't Madonna walk through walls?' asked Cary.

'Because she was a material girl living in a material world,' said Charlotte.

'Got it in one,' laughed Cary.

'OK Charlotte, this is your mission if you choose to accept it,' said Martin.

'I'm listening,' laughed Charlotte.

'For the rest of the evening you are Madonna, and we are your dancers, and we will do anything for our star,' said Martin.

'You have the silliest thoughts,' said Charlotte.

'Silly? I'm intrigued,' said Cary.

'So am I,' said Evangeline.

'So, it's OK, Evie?' asked Cary.

She smiled.

The three others looked at Charlotte as she entertained the suggestion, a small smile forming in the corner of her mouth.

'Come on, tell us your thoughts, Charlotte,' said Cary.

'I've obviously had too much Camille Giroud Bourgogne,' said Charlotte.

'You could never have too much red wine,' laughed Cary, filling up her glass again.

'Tell us,' said Martin. 'Tell us your secrets. Tell us something you have told no one else.'

Charlotte giggled and was then silent for a moment.

'Well, I had only ever seen Ray naked. I had never seen another naked man,' she said.

'Your wish was my command,' said Martin, removing his tie and loosening his shirt.

'I was game,' said Cary, following Martin's lead and taking off his sports coat.

The women giggled, their laughter filling the air. The sight of a naked man had a touch of inherent comedy. Martin glanced at Charlotte, who gave him an encouraging nod as he stood there in his satin boxers. In no time, Martin and Cary stood naked in front of a grand baroque mirror.

Evangeline and Charlotte giggled as they ate their dessert while watching the men. Charlotte's eyes widened in surprise as she noticed the black Le Coq Gaulois tattooed on Martin's arm. The women covered their eyes and then cautiously peeked between their fingers, curiosity getting the better of them. Both men stood proudly, their lean and muscular frames on full display, unbothered by their lack of clothing.

'Could I touch you both?' asked Charlotte. 'Was that OK Evie?'
Evie nodded.
'Madonna would never say that,' said Martin.
'What would she say?' asked Charlotte.
'Get your ass over here,' laughed Cary.
'OK, both of you. Get your asses over here,' laughed Charlotte.

Martin and Cary strolled over and stood in front of Charlotte. Her fingertips lightly traced along each man, feeling the roughness of their skin. Her touch elicited an instant response. As they moved closer, the sound of their breathing grew louder.

'What would Madonna do?' asked Martin.

Charlotte firmly grasped the buttocks of both men, relishing the sensation of their firm muscles beneath her touch.

'What does Cary like, Evie?' asked Charlotte.

'He likes it if I take charge,' said Evangeline with a smile.

Martin stroked the side of Charlotte's face.

'Did I say you could touch me?' Charlotte scolded Martin.

'That's more Madonna-like,' said Cary.

'Now both of you remove my clothes for me,' said Charlotte.

The two men worked together, their hands deftly unbuttoning and removing Charlotte's clothes. Martin unbuttoned her blouse with a gentle touch, his fingers grazing against her skin. Charlotte stood, and Martin unzipped her skirt, revealing her bare legs. Cary removed Charlotte's delicate, black lace panties.

'What now, Madonna?' asked Martin.

'Martin, you go down on me while Cary licks my nipples,' said Charlotte barely audibly.

Cary glanced at Evangeline, who nodded in agreement. Cary then leaned down and sensually tasted Charlotte's left nipple while teasingly caressing her right nipple with his hand. Evangeline lightly caressed his buttock with her fingertips.

Martin positioned himself on all fours while Charlotte straddled him, her legs firmly wrapped around his shoulders. She pressed herself against his face, moving rhythmically as he pleasured her with his tongue. With a delicate touch, Martin's tongue caressed the softness between her thighs. His kisses on her inner thighs made her bite her lip and arch her back, eliciting a long sigh of pleasure that escaped her lips.

'I always wondered what Madonna would look like when she had an orgasm,' said Cary.

'Now you know,' said Martin.

WINE

Elke savoured a sip of her red wine, while Martin's intense gaze remained fixed on her, his fingers hovering over the chessboard.

The restaurant they were in, perched on the seventh floor of the building, offered stunning views of Paris through the intricate wooden frame of pergolas covered in grapevines. According to hearsay, the head chef would craft his own wine using these grapes, having the waitresses crush them with their dainty, bare feet.

Elke had her legs crossed, her checked mini skirt hugging her figure. Martin could not help but notice the other men in the restaurant stealing glances at her.

'Well, tell me, Martin, were you successful?' asked Elke.

'Charlotte and Raymond were both relatively easy to seduce,' says Martin, moving his knight.

'And Raymond spanked Zoe?'

'Yes, of course.'

'And you performed oral sex on Charlotte?'

'Why do you doubt me?'

'I'm surprised. Those two always seemed very up tight to me. I would have taken them to be very conservative with sex.'

'All I can say is that your challenge was completed.'

'A toast to you,' said Elke, raising her glass to Martin. He raised his glass, and they clink. 'And how is my rival?'

'Zoe is doing fine.'

'She's such a sweet and innocent girl,' said Elke.

'She is. And now it's time for you to accept my challenge.'

'And how long will we continue this game?' asked Elke.

'Like this game of chess, we will continue until there is a victor or one player concedes.'

'You know I will never concede.'

'Then we will need to have a victor.'

'And the victor will have control of the vanquished?'

'That is what we agreed.'

'And what is the challenge you have in mind for me?'

'Cary is having a get together with his old university friend. They meet occasionally to play chess.'

'Yes?'

'Cary has asked me to spice things up for him. He knows I'm somewhat of a connoisseur when it comes to that sort of thing.'

'You want me to be the spice?'

Martin nodded slightly, his lips curling into a faint smile.

'The instructions are in this envelope.'

'How mysterious,' said Elke, taking Martin's knight with her pawn.

While walking along the Seine, Elke had dug into her pocket and tore open the envelope and read Martin's handwriting. He still liked to use a fountain pen. His handwriting was elegant.

Dear White Queen, you want to control my world and I want to control yours. Will we ever find a way to ease this lingering tension?

As Elke read on, she savoured the sensation of a light breeze rustling through her hair.

'Oh Martin, you mischievous man child,' Elke sighed as she read on.

Elke made a quick stop at a costume store to purchase a black plastic mask, just as Martin had instructed in his letter. Next on her shopping list was a pleated black skirt, black thigh-high stockings and a sheer black blouse.

When she got back to her apartment, she eagerly tried on the outfit and experimented with various wigs, but ultimately settled on a sleek black bob that perfectly complemented the ensemble. Elke meticulously applied long, fluttering false eyelashes. She carefully wrapped a scarf around the wig, ensuring that it looked natural.

Martin and Zoe were waiting for her in a taxi on Rue de Monttessuy, outside her apartment at seven pm. Elke noticed Zoe was wearing a long raincoat, its fabric swishing softly with each step.

'Give me a peek at what you have under that,' said Elke.

Zoe flashed a quick smile, her lips curving into a mischievous grin, and then opened the raincoat. She wore clothing like Elke, but her outfit was all white, and she had a white bobbed wig. Her impossibly high white heels clicked and clacked upon the pavement.

In Cary's apartment, the chessboard was laid out meticulously as Cary and his old friend Antoine prepared for the game. They sat at the table, swirling their glasses of cognac, and puffing on cigars. The apartment had a balcony, and right next to it, there was a table and chairs. On the opposite side of the street, an elderly gentleman sat on his balcony, quietly observing the passersby.

'Evening gentlemen,' said Martin when he entered the apartment.

Both women hung their raincoats neatly on the hooks by the door.

'Zoe, you look amazing,' said Cary.

'Thank you,' said Zoe.

'And who is your beautiful friend?'

'You've not met Elke before?'

'I don't think I have. I'm sure I would remember someone so beautiful,' said Cary. 'Come meet Antoine.'

Antoine stood and shook the hand of Zoe and Elke.

'Do you always dress like this?' asked Antoine.

'No, they were the instructions,' said Elke.

'The instructions for what?' asked Antoine.

Martin looked at Elke and Zoe and placed his finger to his lips.

'Where's Evangeline?' asked Martin.

'She's visiting her parents in the country,' said Cary.

Martin nodded.

'Just as well. I don't think she would approve,' Martin said.

'What are you talking about?' asked Antoine.

'Two sides, thirty-two pieces, sixty-four squares,' said Martin.

'Are you talking about chess? Why would Evangeline not approve of chess?'

'Start your game gentlemen and call out your move,' said Martin who nodded to Zoe and Elke.

Elke took a seat on one side of the lounge and Zoe on the other. They faced each other across the room. A black-and-white checkered rug was on the floor between them laid out like a chessboard.

'Wow. A chessboard rug. You boys must really love your chess,' said Elke.

'White pawn in front of queen two places,' said Cary.

Martin looks at the two women and said, 'Mesdames, you know what to do.'

Zoe stood up and took two steps forward.

'Black pawn in front of queen two places,' said Antoine.

Elke also stood up and took two steps towards Zoe.

'White pawn to F4,' said Cary.

Elke stepped to the side.

'Black pawn takes white pawn,' said Antoine.

'As black has taken a white piece, Zoe must remove one item of clothing,' said Martin. 'Antoine, you choose what piece of clothing Zoe must remove.'

Antoine swallowed and looked at the beautiful, slender Zoe, looking slightly embarrassed by the scenario.

'Zoe, darling, could you please remove your bra?' Antoine asked then took a sip from his glass as Zoe turned away so that her back was to the three men, and unhooked her white lace bra, pulled it out and placed it on the coffee table.

All three men looked at Zoe's blouse closely to see the nipple and areola of each breast standing prominently against the soft white silk blouse. Her breasts looked firm like two fresh apples, fresh and firm with ruby puckering nipples. To Cary she looks incredibly seductive, like Venus De Milo come to life.

'What size are they?' asked Cary.

'The size of her nipples?'

'Yes.'

'I would say the size of a ladybird,' says Martin.

'Can she orgasm just from nipple stimulation?' asked Cary.

'She can orgasm just by you looking at her,' laughed Martin.

Antoine looked embarrassed, as did Zoe. Her cheeks were flushed red, and she looked down at her shirt and is ashamed to see that her nipples were poking forward even further from the crude way that Martin was talking about her.

Damn this stupid game, she thought but did not dare say anything. To say anything out of turn would break the rules of the game.

'Next move, Antoine,' said Martin.

'White bishop to C4,' said Cary.

Zoe stepped twice to the side.

'Black queen to H4,' said Antoine. 'Check.'

Elke moved forward.

'White king to F1.'

Zoe took a step to the side.

'Black pawn to C5,' said Antoine.

Elke stepped forward two steps.

'White bishop takes black pawn,' said Cary.

'OK Cary, what item of clothing would you like Elke to remove?'

'I don't know. You choose,' said Cary sheepishly.

'I am the game master. I cannot choose,' said Martin. 'Cary, what is it going to be?'

Cary looked at Elke, waiting patiently for his instruction with a half-smile on her bright red lips.

'Her panties,' said Cary after a long pause.

'Bold choice,' said Martin.

Elke smiled, flashing her perfect white teeth.

'OK Cary, Elke needs some help. Why don't you remove them for her?' said Martin.

Cary stepped forward away from the chess table and reached up under Elke's skirt. Her skin was soft and warm. She smelled of lavender. He found the top of her panties and pulled them down her legs, and she stepped out of them.

'Let me see them,' said Martin.

Cary handed the black lace panties to Martin, and he held them up to the light.

'There's not much to them, is there?' said Martin.

'Does Elke normally wear such beautiful underwear, Martin?' asked Cary.

'I'm surprised she is wearing any,' snorted Martin.

Elke shot him a withering look. She too did not want to breach the rules of the game. That would mean that Martin automatically won the round.

'Black knight to F6,' said Antoine.

The two men made several moves each on the board without another piece being taken until a black pawn took a white bishop.

'Which piece of clothing would you like Zoe to remove, Antoine?' asked Martin.

Antoine looked at Zoe, considering his options.

'Choices, choices,' he said. 'I would love to see those beautiful long legs in all their glory. Her skirt.'

Zoe unclipped her skirt and meticulously folded it, the soft fabric smooth against her fingertips, before placing it over the back of a chair. As she resumed her position on the chessboard, the men's eyes locked onto her with intense curiosity. She glanced at Martin, a wry smile playing on his lips. It felt like just yesterday when she met him, standing outside his grand house in Paris, hoping to secure a job as his maid to support her college education. She was now immersed in her studies for her masters, while trying to navigate her complicated relationship with Martin, who was both her boyfriend and Elke's long-term lover. However, she had reached a point where she no longer wanted to share him. The thought of having Martin all to herself consumed her. That is why the game held such significance. Zoe gave Martin an ultimatum, and he gave her a game to resolve it. In the game, the rules dictated players would take turns challenging each other, and a single failure would result in losing the game. Elke presented Martin and Zoe with a series of challenges, while Martin reciprocated by creating challenges for Elke. If Elke emerged victorious, Zoe would be forced to bid farewell to Paris and surrender to Elke's authority. Conversely, if Zoe claimed victory, Elke would be obligated to comply with her desires, even if it meant prohibiting any contact with Martin unless commanded.

Zoe issued Martin an ultimatum, and he retaliated by burdening her with this ridiculous game - obliging her to conquer each challenge, regardless of how distasteful or embarrassing. How could she even know that Martin was being sincere? She scrutinized his facial expressions for any signs of deception. What if she won the game, but Martin still could not commit to her? She often pondered the serenity she would experience if it were just her and Martin, without Elke's constant interruptions. At the bottom of her heart, Zoe loved Martin despite all his flaws and idiosyncrasies. He was the bastion against the solitude in her life. Life seemed like a never-ending cycle of greyness, boredom, and predictability before she met Martin. Now she felt invigorated, living life on the precipice, and appreciated. She was still the same person she always was, but now she commanded the attention of everyone around her. Even while playing Martin's game, she possessed a captivating allure that enticed others.

'Her legs are amazing, Martin,' said Cary. 'Don't you agree, Antoine?'

Antoine's gaze travelled from Zoe's high-heeled shoes to her perfectly styled hair, and he nodded approvingly.

'How would you rate them out of ten, Antoine?' asked Martin.

'You're a lucky man, Martin. A ten,' said Antoine.

'White bishop to F4 to take the black pawn,' said Cary.

'OK Cary, which item of clothing would you like Elke to remove?'

'Her skirt,' said Cary.

Elke slowly unbuttoned her skirt, exposing her cute bottom, and the neatly trimmed pubic hair below. Her long legs were further enhanced by the elegant combination of high heels and thigh-high black stockings.

'Black queen to white pawn,' said Antoine.

'Clothing item?' asked Martin.

'Her blouse,' said Antoine. 'I want to see them.'

Zoe unbuttoned her blouse, feeling the cool air against her bare skin.

'Wow,' said Antoine. 'May I ask what size they are?'

'Size 40,' said Zoe.

'Smile please Zoe when you are talking to Antoine.'

With a subtle raise of her eyebrows, Zoe flashed a quick, knowing smile.

'Walk over here so Antoine can examine them more closely,' said Martin.

With each stride, Zoe's high heels echoed through the room as she approached Cary and Antoine.

'They are even more spectacular up close,' said Antoine. 'Firm like two succulent oranges.'

'OK. OK. Let's proceed with the game. Stop waxing lyrical over Zoe's breasts.'

'White bishop to black knight,' said Cary.

'OK, now let's move to the next level,' said Martin.

'What's that?' asked Antoine.

'You cannot only ask Elke to remove an item of clothing, you can request her to do anything,' said Martin.

'Anything?' queried Cary.

'Yes, anything,' said Martin.

'I would like her to squeeze and pull her nipples,' said Cary.

Elke gently pulled on her nipples, elongating her breasts and feeling a rush of pleasure.

'Beautiful,' said Cary.

'Black bishop to white castle,' Antoine said.

'What's it going to be, Antoine?' asked Martin.

'I want to see Zoe lick Elke's face,' said Antoine.

Elke walked over to Elke and affectionately licked her face, leaving a wet trail from her chin to her forehead.

'White queen to F6.'

'Black knight takes white queen,' Antoine said.

'Now what would you wish for Zoe to do?'

'I want to see her intimately. I want her to part her lips and show me what she looks like deep inside,' said Antoine.

Zoe hesitated, her hand hovering in mid-air, unsure of what lay ahead. Who does he think he is? - she wondered, perplexed by his arrogance. Martin nodded, and then Zoe squatted down on the rug, feeling the soft fibres beneath her as she spread her legs apart.

'Incredible,' said Antoine.

'What is it like to be with her, Martin?' asked Cary.

'She is amazing. Enthusiastic and unrestrained, like a wildcat,' said Martin.

'I can see how wet she is,' said Antoine. 'This is certainly getting her horny.'

'She's always horny. Wants it twenty-four seven. Always wet and ready for it,' said Martin.

'Is that right, Zoe?' asked Cary.

With a shy glance at Cary, Zoe remained silent, yet her vulva shimmered with anticipation.

'White bishop to E7,' said Cary. 'Check.'

'That's checkmate, isn't it?' said Antoine.

'It is,' said Cary.

The sound of Antoine's king hitting the table echoed through the room.

'Elke, your kingdom has fallen,' said Martin. 'You are now the black king's slave. Do you understand?'

Elke nodded.

'What are you going to do with her, Antoine?' asked Martin.

'First, I want her to help Zoe out,' Antoine said, then took a long drink from his glass.

'What do you mean?' asked Martin.

'The poor girl is desperate for some attention,' said Antoine. 'Zoe, you come sit up here on the table next to the chessboard with your legs apart.'

With each step, Zoe's hips swayed enticingly as she walked over in her high white heels. Cary extended his hand, helping her climb onto the table behind the chessboard.

'Good girl,' says Antoine, examining Zoe's flawless thighs above her white stockings and the delicate folds between her legs.

'Now Elke you come over here and lean over this table, with your bottom high in the air and your head right here on the chessboard,' says Antoine.

Elke sauntered over on her high heels, capturing the attention of all three men. Her lower back arched gracefully, accentuating her soft, shapely rump.

'And Elke spread those legs apart behind you,' said Antoine. 'Further, please. That's better.'

Elke could feel the eyes of all three men upon her, taking in her long legs and shapely bottom. Her head rested on the chessboard between

Zoe's legs. Cary reached his hand out and stroked Elke's buttock, his hand sliding over her sweet soft curves then cupping it to feel the weight of it. He then pinched her bottom, causing her to startle and look back at Cary with a look that could kill. Cary laughed.

Antoine got a rubber band and shot it across at Elke's other buttock.

'Now lick up and down, Elke. Think of a cat licking cream from a plate. But do it slowly. Slowly,' said Antoine.

As Elke's tongue glided along the soft lips between Zoe's thighs, Zoe let out a soft murmur of pleasure. Antoine picked up the white king from its place next to Elke, its smooth surface glinting in the light.

'Elke, did you know what this was?'

Elke looked over at the chess piece, feeling the weight of it in her hand.

'Don't stop,' whispered Zoe, biting her lower lip.

'Don't worry, sweetheart. She'll get back to you in a moment. Just that you couldn't have all the fun. So, Elke, did you know what this was?'

'The white king,' said Elke. 'So?'

'This was your master,' said Antoine. 'You had to do everything he said.'

'He was just a carved piece of wood painted white.'

'That was like saying the Mona Lisa was just some colored oil on board,' said Antoine.

Cary and Martin burst into laughter.

'Kiss it,' said Antoine, holding the white king in front of Elke's lips.

Elke's eyes remained fixated on the chess piece, examining every delicate detail.

'They were the rules of the game, Elke,' said Martin.

With a touch of hesitation, Elke pursed her lips and delicately kissed the chess piece.

'Now open up,' said Antoine.

Elke tore her gaze away from the white king, her eyes searching the room for another point of focus.

'You didn't have to, Elke, if you didn't want to,' said Zoe, stroking Elke's hair.

Cary's hand connected with Elke's bare buttock, creating a resounding slap. Elke's eyes widened in disbelief. Laughter erupted from Martin and Cary, filling the air with their infectious mirth.

'You belonged to the white king,' said Antoine. 'Say it.'

'I belonged to the white king,' said Elke, looking down at the chessboard.

'OK, now open up,' said Antoine.

As Elke parted her lips, Antoine slid the white king piece inside her mouth.

'Now show your appreciation of the white king and how much pleasure he gives you,' said Antoine.

Elke let out a soft moan as the chess piece slid in and out of her mouth.

'She was really getting into it,' said Cary.

'Now don't forget about Zoe. Use your fingertips to stimulate her clit,' said Antoine.

Elke gently caressed Zoe's delicate flower bud with her fingertips.

'And show us what you would like the white king to do to your clit,' said Antoine.

As Antoine kept moving the chess piece in and out of Elke's mouth, she reached back between her legs, savoring her own sensations.

'Now hold the white king between your teeth and bring Zoe to orgasm with him while still stroking your own clit. The white king has the power to bring you both to climax,' said Antoine.

With the chess piece in hand, Elke skilfully pleasured Zoe by simultaneously stimulating her clit and penetrating her. Zoe let out a low moan. Zoe's body quivered with delight as Elke expertly pleasured her with her mouth and fingers. Cary's hand gently caressed the curve of Elke's buttock. He could sense her pleasure as she shuddered and nearly lost her balance.

'We're not finished with you yet, Elke.' Antoine's voice carried a hint of menace.

CAFE

Elke and Martin sat at Les Deux Magots café in Saint-Germain des Prés, savouring the aroma of freshly brewed coffee and croissants, as they embraced the chilly winter breeze on the terrace. The narrow streets around the cafe were filled with people clad in dark clothing, bustling about. Elke's legs were crossed, and the fishnet stockings she wore added a touch of edginess to her outfit. Despite the bags under her eyes from lack of sleep, she looked stunning. The previous night had been long and exhausting.

'What did you think of last night's challenge?' asked Martin.

'I wouldn't have expected anything less perverted from you, Martin,' said Elke, sipping from her coffee cup.

'We were even now. Did you still want to proceed further with the game?' Martin asked.

'How would we have ever settled everything without the game? We would have been lost,' said Elke.

'Were we ever found to begin with?'

'I guess not.'

'Did Zoe want to proceed with the game?'

'She wanted me not to see you anymore. She wanted me all to herself,' said Martin.

'Would one woman ever have been enough to satisfy you, Martin?'

'If she was a woman with similar appetites to me,' said Martin.

'A nymphomaniac.'

'There was nothing wrong with enjoying sex.'

'You thought about it twenty-four hours a day though.'

'But didn't we all? Weren't you just like me? Hungry for the next experience.'

'I didn't think everyone else thought about it the way we did.'

'And how was that?'

'As sport.'

'You passed my last challenge. Will Zoe and I pass yours?'

'A very important man is visiting Paris in secret.'

'Who?'

'Of course, I cannot say.'

'How do you know?'

'Well, he likes to have the most beautiful models in Paris at his parties.'

'How does he keep his party secret? He's not the man you want to get on the wrong side of.'

'Why are you even mentioning him to me?'

'That's the challenge. You and Zoe sneak into this party and you get this man into a uniform and get Zoe to get naked with nothing on but her black Louboutins with him while you candidly take photographs of them together.'

'Elke, this sounds dangerous to me,' said Martin.

'So?'

'It's an escalation in the game.'

'Wait until you see who the man is.'

'What if I refuse to go to this little get together?'

'Then you lose the game, and you have to say goodbye to Zoe and I have you all to myself again.'

'I hate to lose a game,' said Martin.

'So, you're in?'

'I'm in.'

'How should we dress?'

'Zoe, as I mentioned should be nude apart from her shoes and a black mask. She can wear a sheer black dress. Some nice diamond earrings would be nice and a diamond necklace. My friend likes bling. Also, a fascinator with black lace would do nicely. Oh, and ensure she has bright red lipstick, false eyelashes, and black mascara.'

'What should I wear?'

'Black tuxedo, black shirt, and a black mask. Also, don't be surprised if the guest of honour brings out a riding crop, a harness, and a saddle.'

'I don't understand.'

'Whose game is this?'

'Yours. How do we get through the door?'

'I have the password.'

'Which is?'

'Whatever is done for love always occurs beyond good and evil.'

'Friedrich Nietzsche?'

'Yes. You know it is still an hour until I'm due on the catwalk.'

'What are you suggesting?'

'Wait a moment, then follow me downstairs.'

'Where are you going?'

'To the ladies.'

'You want me to join you in the ladies?'

'Yes, be careful.'

Martin's eyes followed Elke's every move as she leisurely walked into the inviting cafe. He never tired of watching her walk - the graceful sway of her hips, accentuated by the tight dress that revealed every perfect curve.

After paying the bill, Martin made his way down the stairs to the dimly lit basement toilet area. He waited a few moments, but there was no sign of movement or sound coming from the toilet area. Just as he reached the entrance of the women's toilets, a woman exited, momentarily blocking his way.

'Pardon,' said Martin, attracting a baffled look from the woman before she ascended the stairs.

Once the woman had departed, Martin hesitantly stepped into the bathroom, the sound of his footsteps echoing off the tiled walls.

'Oh,' he heard Elke sigh behind one of the toilet doors.

'Have you started without me?'

As Martin opened the door, he was confronted with an unexpected and intimate sight - Elke sitting on the toilet, her dress hitched up, lost in her own pleasurable world.

'You are horny,' said Martin, just watching her pleasure herself.

'You know this is how I get ready for a show,' panted Elke.

'Show me,' said Martin.

In the cramped toilet cubicle, Elke used her fingers to hold her labia apart, inviting Martin to look inside. Martin slipped his hand between Elke's legs. She felt warm and wet.

'Play while you take me with your mouth,' said Martin.

With a sly grin, Elke lifted her gaze to meet his, a mischievous glint in her eyes. Martin's excitement was so intense that he felt like he might burst out of his trousers just from that look. Elke unzipped his fly with one hand and took out his penis and put it in her mouth while stroking herself with the other hand. Her mouth enveloped Martin, and she could feel him growing and hardening against her tongue. As someone else entered the bathroom, the sound of the door creaking echoed through the tiled room. Despite Elke's best efforts to be silent, the other woman caught the faintest sound of their presence.

Martin slowly unbuttoned Elke's blouse, revealing a glimpse of her delicate skin underneath. He felt himself teetering on the edge of ecstasy, causing Elke to pause and glance up at him.

'You know I really can't get enough of you. Could you really stand life without me?'

Martin's mind went blank, unsure of how to respond.

Elke squeezed Martin's penis tightly with her hand and said, 'Now take me like an animal.'

Elke then stood up from the toilet seat, feeling the cool porcelain against her thighs, and turned around, pressing her bare skin against Martin's throbbing excitement. Her body quivered and contorted in response to his deep penetration, a mix of pleasure and unease surging through her. With a firm grip, he traced the contours of her bare hips, relishing the velvety smoothness of her skin.

INVITATION

Martin and Zoe strolled through central Paris, their footsteps echoing on the cobblestone streets as they passed the majestic Gothic curves of the Notre-Dame de Paris. It stood there, closed to the public, as the sounds of construction work filled the air. The rain fell in heavy droplets, drenching everything in sight.

As they walked up the steps to the club, Martin protected Zoe from the rain with a large, black umbrella. Martin's astonishment grew as he and Zoe were allowed entry into Le Paon Dansant, an exclusive nightclub in the seventh arrondissement, without being questioned by the two bouncers, both donning stylish Ermenegildo Zegna suits. Zoe's eyes glimpsed a masked man, his hand tightly gripping a golden thread that was connected to a dazzling diamond necklace. Nearby, a stunning young woman stood, her sheer dress revealing her naked form.

They entered through a grand archway towering above them. All the women at the party were dressed in the same elegant manner as Zoe. All the men were dressed in sleek, tailored dinner suits, exuding an air of sophistication. The women exuded beauty, their vibrant presence contrasting with the enigmatic men who seemed indistinguishable from one another. They were all sipping on glasses of bubbly champagne. Zoe's curiosity piqued as she wondered about the contents of the black velvet bag slung over Martin's shoulder.

Elke's whereabouts remained a mystery, but Martin's gaze fell upon a duo of old Russian business associates. Most of the people there were speaking in rapid-fire Russian, creating a lively buzz of conversation. The lighting in the private club was low, casting a soft glow over the surroundings. A DJ filled the room with a subtle blend of electro-ethnic rhythms and tribal beats. As she entered the large room, she was struck by its dark and elegant ambiance. Above the dance floor, a grand vaulted ceiling towered overhead, creating an expansive atmosphere. The room was lined with large potted palms, creating a lush and green atmosphere.

As the guest of honour entered the room, the crowd erupted into applause. He wore a full Venetian mask, concealing his identity completely. His silhouette had a familiar shape that triggered a sense of recognition in Zoe. The man, standing alone, surveyed the room filled with women before making his way towards Zoe.

'Good evening, my darling,' the guest whispered in a Russian accent. 'May I?'

'Be my guest,' replied Martin.

Zoe did not dare look at the guest and looked to the floor.

The guest moved his hands over Zoe, tracing along her hips, circling around her buttocks and then down her legs.

'My name is Fedya. What is your name?'

That's how she knew him. He's Fedya Volkov, the Russian oligarch who was otherwise known as the Wolf.

'I'm Zoe.' she said shyly.

'You are breathtaking, my love,' Fedya whispered, his hands delicately caressing Zoe's chest, coaxing her nipples to stand erect beneath the sheer fabric. The other couples had formed a circle around them, their eyes fixed on Fedya shamelessly touched Zoe. As Fedya talked to her, he continued to touch Zoe's breasts.

'You live here in Paris, my darling?'

'Yes, I grew up here,' said Zoe.

'A delightful city,' said Fedya.

'I bet you were popular with the boys?'

'Not really.'

'I'm surprised. Very surprised, my darling.'

Fedya's hands now explored the curves of her waist, tracing along her toned abdomen. As he lifted the hem of her sheer black dress, Zoe could feel the warmth of Fedya's touch on her bare buttocks. His fingers leisurely wandered along the softness of her thighs, leaving a trail of anticipation in their wake.

'If I was a young man on the streets of Paris and saw you, I would have given anything just to have you smile at me,' said Fedya, his fingers stroking Zoe's pubic hair.

'I like the way you have shaved your pubic hair. I like the way it frames your inner petals. Very sexy, wouldn't you agree ladies and gentlemen?'

Approving nods and murmurs rippled through the crowd. Zoe held her breath as Fedya's finger delicately traced her labia, moving in a gentle, rhythmic motion. She stood stiffly, her body tense and unmoving. Zoe blushed as the stranger's hand grazed her arm in the bustling crowd.

Fedya's fingers delicately parted her lips as she grew wet. His touch sent a gentle, warm shiver down her spine, igniting a sense of arousal. He had the touch of an expert, his fingers gliding effortlessly across her genitalia. He prided himself on being a connoisseur of women, able to appreciate their unique beauty and charm. His touch was delicate, yet it conveyed a sense of strength. He revelled in the silky smoothness of her skin. The pace was slow and calm, as if time itself had slowed down.

Zoe moved her pelvis in a seductive rhythm as Fedya skilfully explored her with his fingers. As she moves, her breasts sway against the sheer black dress, their firmness clear through the fabric. She feels a mix of embarrassment and excitement coursing through her. She hears the faint sound of her own whimper escape her lips. One thing she knows is that she does not want to lose the warmth of Fedya's touch. Fedya delicately takes her hand and guides it to explore the intimate space between her legs.

'Darling, please continue,' Fedya says. 'You're adorable.'

Zoe looks around the room at all the people staring at her through their masks. Who are these people? Is my professor amongst them? My neighbor? My doctor? She then sees Elke who nods. I must not lose the game, thinks Zoe and then moves her hand between her legs in the most intimate way possible, squeezing her labia together before stimulating her soft bud of pleasure. She can feel how aroused she is. Like she is coming apart and will just dissolve on the floor. Can everyone else notice?

'Don't come yet, my darling,' says Fedya. 'Just keep yourself on that edge. But please taste your arousal.'

Zoe looks around the room again and her eyes meet Elke's. She knows she must comply and brings her hand up to her lips and licks her hand.

'Put your hand in your mouth. Revel in the taste of your arousal,' says Fedya.

Zoe moves two fingers into her mouth and sucks upon them. The taste of her skin is salty.

'I bet you taste sweet,' says Fedya.

'OK now return to stroking yourself. Just do it slowly and don't allow yourself to climax. I want everyone to appreciate your beauty.'

'Come everyone. Feel these amazing breasts while this beautiful young woman pleasures herself. You must try to make her climax by stroking her breasts and nipples while she strokes herself and tries to resist climaxing.'

This is insane, thinks Zoe to herself yet still she doesn't stop stroking. In an attempt to distract herself, she focuses on the latest chapter of her PhD, the pile of emails waiting for her response, and the sight of her dirty car.

Each couple approaches her, their footsteps echoing in the silence, as Fedya watches closely. Zoe noticed a bald Russian man and his stunning Italian wife approaching her. His rough hands forcefully grasp Zoe's breast, treating her as if she were his possession. The wife delicately caresses the other nipple, savouring the sensation. Despite the incredible sensations, Zoe stays composed.

'Next,' says Fedya.

With a tinge of disappointment, the bald man reluctantly rejoins the other couples. His partner sashays back into the circle, her high heels clicking with each sway.

The next couple comprises a young man with a trendy, short haircut and tattoos adorning his neck, accompanied by his girlfriend with flowing, golden locks and a confident posture. The man nods to Zoe, and his partner indulges in a sensual display, alternating between sucking one nipple and stroking the other gently with her hand, while her partner tenderly strokes her behind. His hand ventures under the sheer dress, grasping and squeezing each buttock with confidence.

'Come on baby, make her come. Let's win this game,' says the young man.

There must be more than just us playing this game, thinks Zoe.

The blonde's sucking and rubbing became more intense, causing Zoe to adjust her own pace to prevent herself from climaxing too soon.

'OK you two. That's enough. Move on,' says Fedya.

'Baby, we were so close,' says the young man.

'I'm sorry, sweetheart. I did my best,' says the blonde.

'I know you did, baby,' says the young man is touching the blonde on the behind.

Zoe continues to stroke between her legs, feeling the growing heat and anticipation. It is Elke, but she does not recognize the man, a young, muscled man of Algerian background.

'You look delectable,' whispers Elke into Zoe's ear. 'You know that with just one stroke of that delicate nub you can be free of this game. Free of Martin and join me and experience endless pleasure with me. I would treat you very well, not like Martin treats you. You should give up now. Things will get much worse for you if you do not surrender to pleasure now.'

'I'm going to win this game,' says Zoe, slightly out of breath as Elke uses a light touch to circle Zoe 's breasts and areola with large strokes, then does a little squeeze of each breast.

The Algerian then moves in closer, his fingertips gently tracing her areola, creating an intense anticipation that causes Zoe's nipples to grow even harder. His hands, with their broadness and warmth, provided a sense of security and comfort.

The Algerian then caresses Zoe's nipples gently, escalating the intensity and pace. The Algerian then ruthlessly squeezes Zoe's nipples, sending a jolt of sensation coursing through her. Just as Zoe is on the verge of climax, the guest interrupts, shattering the moment.

'Time's up. I'm afraid. You may stop now, my darling. I am impressed with your self-control,' says the guest to Zoe. 'I can see how aroused you are but just hold off for now. Your time to climax will come soon.'

Zoe glanced at the crowd of people in the nightclub, their eyes fixed on her. She is almost delirious with all the sensations.

'You and your man need to come with me upstairs,' says the guest. 'You first, my dear.'

Zoe walks towards the spiral staircase, the soft murmurs of the couples parting to make way for her and Martin. As Zoe steps up the stairs in her high heels, all the couples watch, mesmerised by the sway of her behind.

ROOM

The upstairs area at Le Paon Dansant offered a taste of luxury with its opulent lounge area, featuring inviting red velvet lounges. The area was dimly lit, casting long shadows that made Zoe feel as though the night was creeping closer.

'Please have a seat, my dear,' Fedya said.

'Thank you,' said Zoe, who was barely audible, taking a seat, feeling the soft velvet underneath her, and crossing her legs.

Fedya approached Zoe and fixed a gold collar around her neck.

'Here is a present to you for doing so well with that last challenge,' said Fedya.

'What do you say Zoe?' said Martin.

'Thank you, sir,' whispered Zoe, looking at the floor.

'You have such gracious manners, my darling,' said Fedya.

'She has impeccable manners,' said Martin.

'And I imagine she is amazing in bed,' said Fedya.

'She is incredible. Attentive. Aroused. Always beautiful and caring,' said Martin.

'Let me see my darling,' said Fedya.

'I don't understand,' said Zoe, barely audibly.

'He wants you to open your legs, Zoe,' said Martin.

Zoe uncrossed her legs and placed her hand between them and spread them apart.

'Come now, my darling, we were past the point of modesty.' said Fedya. 'Way past. Open your legs as far apart as you can and proudly display your womanhood. It was a treasure, not something to be hidden. Display it with pride.'

Zoe adjusted her position on the red velvet sofa, spreading her legs wider apart.

'Use your fingers to open your lips,' said Fedya.

Zoe does as she is instructed.

'And smiled. You had such a beautiful smile. So mysterious,' said Fedya.

'That was better,' said Fedya. 'You were literally throbbing with passion.'

Martin leaned in close and whispered something to Fedya, his words barely audible.

'Your man told me you had a secret fantasy. Well, I was more than happy to oblige,' said Fedya.

'Get up and rest your head on the top of the sofa with your legs apart. Stroke yourself slowly but do not come. I need to get changed,' said Fedya.

After a couple of minutes, Fedya said, 'OK, you can turn around now, Zoe.'

Zoe's eyes widened as she saw Fedya, now unmasked, wearing a black uniform and a military-style hat. In his hand, he tightly gripped a riding crop. He stepped towards her, the sound of his footsteps echoing in the silence, and ran the riding crop down the side of her cheek.

'Did I say for you to stop stroking yourself?' said Fedya.

'No, sir,' said Zoe.

'Then get back to it.'

'Yes, sir.'

Zoe's eyes were drawn to the wooden table, adorned with a white tablecloth that seemed to float like a ghost in front of a grand baroque mirror.

'What was that?'

'Go explore, my darling,' said Fedya.

Zoe tentatively pulled the tablecloth, revealing an unexpected sight - an incredibly large, black dildo affixed to the table. She gasped, overwhelmed by the sheer magnitude of it.

'That looked enormous,' she whispered.

'It is, my darling, but I had the feeling that you were ready for it. Take off your heels and get up on the table and take that beast, my darling. Face the mirror and watch yourself. Your handsome partner and I will watch you from behind.'

Zoe gingerly stepped up onto a chair, then onto the table, feeling the smooth surface beneath her feet. She took a deep breath before mounting the dildo, feeling it fill her as she descended.

'It's too big,' whimpered Zoe.

'Grind into the tip, my darling,' said Fedya. 'Do it slowly and watch yourself in the mirror.'

Zoe sensually glided her lips over the sleek, ebony tip of the dildo, moving back and forth in a rhythm that matched her desire. Zoe examined her reflection in the mirror, her eyes resembling deep pools hidden behind her mask. The atmosphere was filled with an air of mystery. The sight of the young woman on the table, pleasuring herself with a large black dildo, left her stunned and unsure of how to react. As she took it, she noticed her chest rise and fall with each breath and felt a knot tighten in her stomach. Her long, flowing hair cascaded down onto her shoulders. Her eyes, wide and unblinking, stared intensely back at her from the reflection. She felt like she was both judging herself and was lost. The angel on one shoulder wondered how she could show herself like this, completely unrestrained. Simply savour the sensation, without judgment or rules, only pure delight, whispered the devil on her shoulder.

Fedya and Martin circled the table, closely observing her as she rhythmically moved up and down on the dildo, gradually taking in more of its length. The bright flashing lights of the club accentuated the pearlescent hue of her buttocks, making them stand out.

'Flawless,' said Fedya. 'Play with your clitoris as you penetrate yourself.'

Zoe supported herself with one hand as she moved up and down on the phallus, her other hand caressing herself with each thrust.

'You're doing so well my darling,' says Fedya. 'Remember not to come yet. Wait until I say.'

Fedya's taps on Zoe's buttocks started off light, gradually growing stronger, mimicking the intensity of a jockey urging their horse towards victory. Zoe let out a loud sigh as she fully embraced the size of the enormous black dildo.

'Good girl,' said Fedya encouragingly. 'I knew you could do it if you tried hard enough. You just needed a little encouragement.'

Zoe struggled to contain her pleasure, finding it incredibly difficult not to reach climax. She gazed at her reflection in the mirror, her hair bouncing playfully with each movement. She could hear Fedya and Martin's footsteps as they walked around her, creating a rhythmic pattern. Fedya approached Zoe and gently touched her breasts, eliciting a mixture of pleasure and pain as he twisted her nipples. Meanwhile, Zoe rode the dildo with an intense fervour, feeling waves of sensation with every thrust. Martin's camera shutter clicked as Zoe, from the corner of her eye, spotted him photographing her and Fedya.

'Now get down off the table, my dear,' said Fedya.

Zoe noticed her legs trembling, causing her to struggle to maintain her balance.

'Darling, put your heels back on,' said Fedya.

Zoe rested one hand on the table as she put one shoe after another back on.

'Now stand straight with your hands behind your back.'

Zoe felt the cold metal of handcuffs being clasped around each hand.

'Now pretend that the dildo is Martin's cock. Demonstrate how lovingly you treat him,' said Fedya.

Worried she would lose her balance, Zoe leaned forward, her hands tightly clasped behind her back. She sensually tasted her own salty arousal as she ran her tongue along the top of the black phallus.

'Show me how much of him you could take in your mouth,' said Fedya.

Zoe opened her mouth around the enormous phallus.

'How does Martin taste?'

Zoe mumbled something under her breath, barely audible. Her heart pounded in her chest, racing like a wild stallion. She felt flustered. She stole a glance at Martin and saw him capturing more photographs with his camera, a mischievous smirk playing on his lips. Zoe's conflicting emotions rose within her as she both despised and felt drawn to this foolish game.

Fedya mounted Zoe from behind, his forceful entry causing her spine to tingle, while the riding crop left a sharp sting on her thigh. She felt an electric current surging through her veins. All her senses came alive. Every part of her pulsed with energy and vitality.

'OK, now you may come, my darling,' said Fedya, releasing into her.

Fedya delighted in the shiver that ran through Zoe's body, from her toes to her forehead, as everything around her momentarily turned blindingly white.

'You have the most delightful quim my darling. We will certainly meet again,' said Fedya, looking down at the poor young woman slumped over the table, lost in bliss.

'Thank you, Martin, for sharing her,' said Fedya.

'It is my pleasure to share her with you,' said Martin.

STREET

The bustling sounds of the city enveloped Martin and Zoe as they strolled along Rue de Rivoli. A mischievous wind playfully lifted Zoe's long plaid skirt, exposing her bright white underwear to the other pedestrians. As tourist ferries glided by on the water, Martin pulled Zoe close, relishing the caress of the gentle breeze on their faces. The sun hung low in the sombre grey sky.

As the rain started to fall, Martin hurriedly opened his umbrella, shielding them from the downpour. Seeking refuge from the intensifying rain, they huddled under the awning of a nearby building. Zoe's eyes locked with Martin's, and in that instant, everything else blurred into insignificance, consumed by their profound connection. Martin gently pressed his lips against Zoe's, savouring the softness and warmth. She often wondered if Martin felt the same rush of emotions as she did. Martin had a wild side, but beneath that, he had a tender and affectionate nature that revealed itself in gentle touches and warm embraces. The look of contentment on his face revealed how much he cherished the warmth and camaraderie. Zoe wondered, why does he persistently challenge me, provoking a constant battle of wits? Reflecting on the night before, she recalled the melodic sound of glasses clinking together and the sight of couples immersed in the game.

Had Martin or Elke agreed to take part in the game to appease Fedya and if so, why? What kind of influence did he have over them? She wanted to ask Martin, but she knew she would only receive evasive responses from him. Whenever the conversation turned serious, he would abruptly shift the topic. He relished in the mystery that surrounded him.

'Why were you taking photographs with your phone last night?' asked Zoe.

'It was part of Elke's challenge,' said Martin. 'I've already sent the photographs to her as proof of the challenge being completed.'

'That's a little unusual, isn't it?'

'Why?'

'She normally just accepts our word for a challenge being completed.'

'We don't analyse the challenge, we just accept the challenge,' said Martin.

'It's all a game to you, isn't it?'

'It is literally a game,' said Martin.

The rain is falling harder.

'I'm jealous of her, Martin. I want you for real.'

'Then set a challenge that Elke cannot complete.'

'I don't know what would be too hard for Elke. She seems up for anything.'

'What is something you find sexy, but that Elke does not?'

'I like it when you play with my feet,' said Zoe. 'Does Elke like that?'

'I certainly like your feet,' said says Martin, wrapping his coat around Zoe to shelter her from the storm.

'You know her better than me, Martin. You must know what a real challenge for her would be,' said Zoe as Martin runs one hand over Zoe's waist and the other over the top of her thighs.

'I would love to take you in the middle of the storm,' said Martin.

'Ssh. There are people everywhere.'

'Your breasts are killing me today. They look so sexy in that black blouse you are wearing,' Martin said, his hand caressing her breast over the blouse.

'Thank you, but don't talk too loudly. There's a man right next to us,' whispered Zoe.

'He's probably insanely jealous of me,' said Martin. 'I don't know which one I like more, the right one or the left one.'

Zoe could feel Martin's hands exploring her body, tracing the contours over her blouse, and his desire pressing against her thigh.

'Stop it, people will see us,' said Zoe.

Martin's fingers lightly grazed her right nipple, creating a tantalizing sensation beneath her blouse and bra.

'I think your right one is my favourite. It likes me more than your left one,' said Martin, leaning forward and kissing Zoe's eyelids and then her lips.

'People are watching,' whispered Zoe as she looks over at the man also sheltering from the storm. He looked away.

'It's all right Zoe. You tell me one thing, but your nipple is telling me something else,' said Martin, touching her breast with slow, rhythmic, and gentle strokes. 'Hold my coat around us.'

Zoe held Martin's coat tightly around them as the rain pounded relentlessly. People passed by them under colourful umbrellas, oblivious to their presence under the awning. But as she felt Martin's other hand running along the top of her leg, she noticed the stranger casting sideways glances at them. She felt Martin's gentle touch on the inside of her thighs, causing them to subtly part, granting him deeper access. He gently brushed her bush with his fingertips, feeling the hair then exploring where her thighs meet. He then pressed his fingers into her, probing her vulva and bottom then finding her clitoris. Martin's other hand unbuttoned her blouse and pushed down her bra cups, freeing her breasts.

'Don't worry about other people, just listen to your body,' whispered Martin in her ear. 'Your body is telling me you want me.'

Zoe's nipples responded to his slow and gentle strokes, becoming more sensitive with each touch. The stranger smiled at her with a strange look of compassion and desire as she pulled Martin's raincoat closer around them as Martin stroked her with abandon on the Paris street. Martin playfully teased her with his fingers before plunging two fingers deep inside her. He rhythmically thrust them in and out of her, causing her hips to twitch uncontrollably. She was embarrassed by how wet and accepting of Martin she was. As she stood there, her breath became shallow, and she had to close her eyes momentarily to regain composure from the overwhelming revulsion and sensations. The urge to protest consumed her thoughts. Despite the urge to cry and weep, she stood there, enveloped in her pleasure.

'I like the rain too,' said the stranger.

HOTEL

Raymond began his address to the gathered shareholders at the Hilton Paris Charles de Gaulle Hotel, just as Elke's shoe slipped off her foot. Hiding behind the podium curtain, she could hear Raymond's every breath. Martin and Zoe sat in the front row, eagerly awaiting the show to begin.

'Good morning, ladies and gentlemen. Welcome to the Annual Meeting for Le Point le Plus Haut. I'm Raymond Garnier, Chairman and CEO.'

Martin's latest challenge for Elke was a collaboration between him and Zoe. Elke's natural personality was one of dominance, always wanting to take charge. She relished the feeling of being in control. This was true in both intimate moments and in everyday experiences. Martin devised the challenge of Elke's complete submission, while Zoe suggested Elke worshiping someone's feet.

Elke gently removed Raymond's sock, revealing his bare foot, and leaned in to sensually caress his big toe with her tongue before taking it into her mouth.

'When I thought about preparing for this... important meeting, I reviewed all the full operational ... and financial data.'

'I want to suck you off,' whispered Elke, looking up at him with a wicked grin.

In the hotel ballroom, Elke's whispered words reached his ears, igniting a sensual charge. Painted in a bold, bright pink hue, her lips appeared full and irresistibly alluring. In a matter of seconds, Raymond's flaccid state transformed into a fully erect one. Martin flashed a warm smile at his friend, while Raymond struggled to maintain his composure. Behind the curtain, only Martin and Zoe were privy to the secret.

'Financially, we have been very disciplined.'

Awkwardly, Elke slipped out of her underwear and tightly held onto Raymond's legs, gradually sinking down onto his big toe until it entered her.

'Your toe is so big,' Elke whispered. 'So hard.'

Elke's clothes clung to her body, drenched from head to toe. With a quiet sigh, she arched her back and rotated her hips in small circles against his toe, seeking pleasure.

Elke then unzipped Raymond's fly, revealing his anticipation, and delicately removed his boxers before embracing him with her warm, inviting mouth. Raymond gently gripped her hair and ran his fingers through it as she skilfully pleasured him. Elke's mouth clung tightly to Raymond's shaft as she increased the intensity of her sucking. Her tongue tantalizingly traced every inch of Raymond's pulsating member as her hand gently cradled his testicles.

Elke stopped sucking for a moment, unbuttoned her blouse, removed her bra, and pressed her breasts around his penis and whispered, 'Come in my mouth.'

Her cheeks turned a deep shade of crimson, revealing her mix of embarrassment and desire. Her nipples stood erect, resembling delicate pink buds. With a playful flick of her tongue, she traced the length of Raymond's shaft, eliciting a shiver of pleasure. Raymond's voice trembled as he struggled to continue speaking to the shareholders. The sensation of Elke's tongue was driving him to the brink of madness. Her mouth eagerly consumed him, her hands exploring his sensitive balls. As she held him, she could feel the rhythm of her heartbeat rocking him back and forth.

'Operationally, we analysed and optimised...'

Raymond glanced downward, observing Elke's rhythmic bobbing on his big toe as she skilfully took him deep into her mouth and throat. Her rump rose and fell upon his feet, creating a rhythmic pattern.

As Raymond held Elke's head close to his abdomen, he could feel the intense rush of sperm coursing through his body and being released.

He arched himself towards her, his body trembling with anticipation as she drained him.

'So the long-term future of the company is... very...ahh..bright.'

The crowd murmured softly, creating a background hum, as Raymond closed his eyes for a moment. Elke murmured softly, and Raymond's body shuddered with pleasure.

Raymond climaxed in silence, leaving the crowd of shareholders puzzled by his unreadable expression. Martin's clapping echoed through the room, gradually drawing in the other shareholders until their applause filled the air with energy.

APARTMENT

Fedya's city apartment, on the third floor of a stunning Haussmann stone building, offered breathtaking views of the Seine and the monuments of the Ile de la Cité. When Elke pressed the intercom to the apartment, she was greeted by Anatoli Anatolyevna, Fedya's bodyguard.

'Yes.'

'It's me,' said Elke.

The apartment door buzzed open, and Elke stepped into the elevator, pressing the button for Fedya's floor. The door swung open, revealing Anatoli standing on the other side. He nodded to Elke as she entered.

'Is this a bad time?' asked Elke.

'Fedya's in the bedroom,' said Anatoli.

'Sleeping?'

'What do you reckon?'

'Don't all vampires sleep during the day?' laughed Elke.

'Hilarious. I wasn't sure if my boss would enjoy being called a vampire,' said Anatoli.

'Where was your sense of humor?'

'I had a sense of humor. I was just messing with you,' Anatoli replied.

The double doors to Fedya's bedroom burst open and a naked young woman with rabbit ears ran out giggling, her breasts bouncing up and down. She quickly covered herself with her hands when she saw Elke.

'Camille, darling, come back,' Fedya said as he walked into the living room, also naked and with a massive erection.

'Elke, are you joining the fun?' Fedya asked.

'I was hoping we could talk,' Elke said.

'Not a problem,' Fedya replied. 'Anatoli, could you please fetch me my dressing gown and some slippers? Camille, could you please go to the bedroom, put your head down on the floor, bottom up, legs spread, and pleasure yourself? I want you to be ready for me when I come back.'

Camille giggled and headed into the bedroom, closing the double doors behind her. After Fedya slipped his dressing gown and slippers on, he sat with Elke at the kitchen table.

'Anatoli, coffee for both of us, please,' Fedya requested. Then he turned to Elke and asked, 'I had been waiting for you to visit.'

'Fedya, I didn't know if I could go on,' Elke said.

'You and Martin were still in my debt. Without me, you both would have been finished. You couldn't pay a debt to the brotherhood.'

'I didn't want to borrow from them. You suggested it and Martin went along with it,' Elke explained.

'Sometimes your options are limited. You and Martin had a problem, and I offered a solution.'

'One that almost got us killed,' Elke stated.

'I got you both out of trouble by guaranteeing your repayment, but you knew that my help did not come without strings,' Fedya said, stroking Elke's cheek with his knuckles.

'I think we have already repaid the favour a thousand times since then,' Elke said indignantly.

'We had an agreement. You would be released from the agreement only when I had what I wanted,' said Fedya, being handed a coffee by Anatoli.

'Why did you want Zoe, though? She was obviously in love with Martin and he had feelings for her, too. Why did you want to break them up? You could have had any woman in Paris you wanted.'

'Zoe was a belle fleur. Martin did not appreciate her. Ever since I saw her on the catwalk, I wanted to possess her. I wanted her to love me as she loved Martin. He did not value beautiful things like I did. He was born into money while I had had to make every cent I had,' said Fedya.

'Martin believed and had told Zoe that the game was being played between him and her and that if they succeeded, then I would stay out of Martin's life and it would just be her and him together - a happy couple,' said Elke. 'I felt bad deceiving both. Martin was my best friend.'

'Martin should have appreciated the sacrifices you had made for him. You did not need to tell them anything, you just needed to win the game. If you won, then Zoe had to leave Martin and submit to you, then you could instruct Zoe to travel to Russia with me and submit to me.'

'Zoe had succeeded in every challenge I had set her. She was determined to win because she loved Martin,' said Elke. 'I didn't see how I could set a challenge that she could not satisfy.'

'Use what she loved to cause her to fail. Use that love to steal her away from him,' said Fedya.

'And how do you propose I do that?'

'The challenge needs to involve hurting Martin. He needs to be totally powerless and humiliated while I ravish and control Zoe in front of the man that she adores.'

'Haven't you already tried that though and Zoe still achieved the challenge?'

'Well, we just have to up the ante, don't we? We must use Zoe's devotion to him to cause her to fail in the task. She will flinch against harming him. Let her virtue and devotion to him be her downfall in the game and free her from a man who is a beast in business and in life. She needs to be thoroughly vanquished in the game to accept her new life as serving you and me. Her instructions are typed on the cards in this envelope.'

MAID

Zoe looked at Martin, glimpsing herself in the rearview mirror with Elke.

Martin's eyes roamed appreciatively over Zoe, unable to hide his awe. From her flowing locks to her mesmerizing eyes filled with intrigue, and her poised and graceful physique, she truly looked extraordinary. Zoe's attire comprised black stockings with a white bow at her mid-thigh, a short lace-trimmed dress with a white apron, a cameo choker collar, a headpiece, a petticoat, and a feather duster, all as per Elke's instructions in the first card of the envelope.

'He's right,' said Elke.

'I looked like a joke. I looked like a frivolous French maid. What was the challenge for that night's episode of the game?' Zoe asked.

'Fedya wanted to see you again. Ever since the other night, he had been obsessed with you. He kept asking me about you,' said Elke.

'What did he want to know?' asked Zoe.

'Where you were born. Your history. How you knew Martin and I,' said Elke.

'Why?'

'You intrigued him.'

'What did you tell him?' asked Zoe.

'That you first met Martin when you took a job as his maid of course and were now a student and model.'

'Was he disappointed?'

'Not at all. He was even more intrigued.'

'How did you know Fedya?'

'He was incredibly wealthy. One of the richest men in the world. A huge number of men worked for him directly or indirectly.'

'You didn't answer my question,' said Zoe.

'Wasn't it my night to be setting the challenge for you?' asked Elke.

'I needed to understand my challenge before I embarked on it.'

'All you need to know is that you are Fedya's gift tonight. The challenge is to submit to his desires no matter how perverse and draw every drop of semen from him. He will call you 'maid' and you will call him 'sir', said Elke. 'You will be the sexual plaything.'

'Don't worry, Zoe. We will be at the party to protect you,' said Martin.

'And determine if you succeed with your challenge,' said Elke.

Martin pulled up at the gates of Fedya's country house, a grand chateau that exuded the elegance of the Belle Epoque era, located just an hour's drive outside of Paris. At the gate, a torch-wielding Russian man scrutinised the three occupants of the car before granting them entry.

Fedya's function was held in the ballroom, which dazzled with gilded mouldings, silk damask walls, sparkling crystal chandeliers, and a gleaming parquet floor that shimmered in the soft candlelight.

Anatoli Anatolyevna, Fedya's bodyguard, stood tall in the doorway, his arms firmly folded across his chest. Zoe's eyes scanned the words on the next card as she pulled it out from the envelope.

'Strip the bouncer naked and bounce on his truncheon like a bunny.'

Zoe looked up at the towering figure of the bouncer standing like a mountain at the entrance to the ballroom. He stood tall over everyone like a giant.

'Excuse me, sir,' said Zoe.

There was no reaction from Anatoli.

'Sir!'

Anatoli's face showed no emotion as he remained still.

As Zoe opened the envelope, a small card slipped out into her palm, and she read its contents once more. 'I must do this or lose the game,' she thought, feeling the weight of the situation settle heavily on her shoulders. With a gentle touch, she unfastened each button on Anatoli's starched white shirt. She had to exert some force to peel it off his well-defined upper body. It was as if she was invisible to him; he didn't even acknowledge her existence. The guests at the party turned their heads, exchanging curious glances at her and Anatoli.

'Lift your foot, please,' said Zoe, gently slipping off Anatoli's shoes, one after the other. She peeled off his socks then unzipped his trousers and then pulled down his jocks.

Anatoli's face remained expressionless, betraying no emotion. He had folded his arms in front again, but the party was murmuring now, filled with an uneasy tension. Anatoli's upright posture accentuated his colossal pole, which seemed like it belonged to a giant. Zoe had never seen a man so big before. 'You know what you must do,' she said to herself, then slowly pulled her own underwear down her legs, revealing her vulnerability to Anatoli. In her high heels, she had to stretch on her tiptoes to reach Anatoli's crotch. He did nothing but stood there, his expression impassive. Zoe's buttocks bounced rhythmically as she rode Anatoli's engorged length. As the friction increased, she could feel him growing larger between her buttocks, sending waves of excitement through her body. However, Anatoli's impassive expression revealed nothing.

The party guests, including Martin, Elke, and Fedya, formed a semi-circle around them, their champagne flutes clinking softly. A joke was cracked, and a ripple of laughter spread through the crowd.

With each motion, Zoe could sense Anatoli's cock becoming slicker, enhancing the pleasure of their intimate connection. Her breasts threatened to spill out of her low-cut bodice. She couldn't bring herself to meet the gaze of all the curious onlookers. She exuded an air of wanton desire. His scent wafted towards her, filling her senses. He exuded a strong, masculine scent, reminiscent of wood and earth.

The party goers commented on the attractiveness of the couple and the high level of effort Zoe was making for Anatoli to enter her. This wanton display of sexuality did not surprise them. It was exactly what they had anticipated from Fedya's parties.

Finally, she could feel Anatoli's hands caressing her delicate skin. She pressed herself against him, her body eagerly pulling him closer, their connection intensifying with every breath. Despite her embarrassment, she could feel herself becoming slick and ready for him. No matter what she had experienced, this remained equally challenging. As Zoe turned to look at him, her eyes locked onto a point in the distance. Her lips, painted a vibrant shade of red, quivered with anticipation as she licked them. Her eyes flickered with a fiery glow. Zoe's heartbeat quickened, pounding in her chest. Her bare buttocks were presented to him on a platter, but he maintained an impassive expression. Zoe pressed herself against him with even more fervour, feeling the strength and heat emanating from his towering figure. It had such a mesmerizing effect on her that the audience couldn't help but be drawn in as well. She appeared consumed by desire, her rationality lost in the moment. It was like the ballroom had become a forest was alive with the sounds of a wild animal in heat, echoing through the trees.

'I needed you inside me,' Zoe pleaded, pressing her inviting entrance up to him, framed by her black corset and long, black-stockinged legs and white frilly petticoats.

She lifted her hips up higher for him and arched herself towards him and breathlessly bucked with great vigour to force him to enter her and then to take more of his giant erection within her, taking more with each thrust onto him, rolling her head and biting her lip, as the fullness of him consumed her. Her inner core became more elastic as she took more of the abundance of him. He was like a white fiery flame melting her, making her quiver with ecstasy from her molten core to the tips of her toes. The prying eyes of the audience disappeared from her mind like smoke. Zoe closes her eyes and wriggles as she impales herself upon him, taking his full length as she makes soft little cries of pleasure. The crowd, seeing that amazingly he is balls deep within her, burst into applause.

STATUE

Zoe hastily pulled up her delicate white panties, desperately trying to regain her composure. She could feel the bouncer's release trickling down her thigh.

'Excuse me, sir, where is the bathroom?' Zoe asked one of the waiters.

'Down there, mademoiselle, near the punch bowl,' said the waiter.

Zoe washed and dried herself in the nether region. Instead of putting on her panties again, she discreetly tucked them away in her handbag. Carefully, she withdrew the next card from the envelope, feeling the smooth texture of the paper against her fingertips. On the card it was written:

'There is a marble statue in the middle of the ballroom. Ask Martin to sit on the chair opposite the statue and remove his clothes. Tie him to the chair with the ropes in the bag under the chair.'

With a heavy sigh, Zoe examined the stack of cards in the envelope. How many additional components were left in this challenge? She read the next card, her eyes scanning the words with curiosity.

'Dry hump the statue, declare that both the bouncer and the statue give more pleasure than Martin and then fake orgasm.'

This was one of the strangest challenges of the game, and she could feel her heart pounding as she contemplated whether to continue. You're on the verge of completing the challenge. She repeated to herself, 'You must go on,' as if the words were a mantra pushing her forward. If she lost the game, she would be forced to part ways with Martin and Paris and become Elke's servant. That is the last thing I would choose; anything else would be preferable. With another sigh, Zoe exited the bathroom and came across Martin. With a firm grip on his hand, she guided him away from the rest of the group.

'Follow me,' she said, wondering if Martin had read the cards before Elke had given the envelope to her.

Martin's hand, warm, held hers as he looked at her with a smile that suggested she had captivated him. Did he expect her to guide him towards an extraordinarily sensual encounter? Some wild, free, and uninhibited sensation. 'Is this what this was?' She wondered.

'Forgive me, Martin,' Zoe whispered as she walked with him to the chair in front of the statue. 'I only want to succeed in the game and claim you as my own.'

As the couple walked towards the statue, a reproduction of David by Michelangelo, the crowd parted, creating a clear path for them. Zoe pondered if the choice of the statue held any hidden meaning. In the Bible, David found himself locked in an intense battle with Goliath. David's muscular physique exuded confidence and perfect proportions. In this battle of the wills, who played the role of David and who assumed the role of Goliath? Zoe envisioned herself as David, the underdog, determined to conquer Elke, whom she perceived as the towering Philistine giant.

'I have agreed to the rules of the game as well, Zoe,' said Martin. 'I too am sorry for what I have put you through. I'm trapped as well. Trapped by my own desires.'

'If I succeed in this game, do you think it is possible for you to settle down with just one woman and be satisfied with that?' asked Zoe.

'If that woman, is you,' Martin said. 'You've very special to me. You've captivated my thoughts since you first came into my life.'

'Strip,' said Zoe when they arrive at the chair in front of the statue of David.

'What?' asked Martin.

'This is the next move in the game,' said Zoe.

'In front of all these people? I know many of these people.'

'If you don't, we will lose the game.'

Martin reluctantly removed his dinner jacket, revealing the faint scent of cologne that clung to the fabric. There was a bag hidden under the chair. Martin then loosened his tie and unbuttoned his dress shirt, feeling the immediate relief as the fabric no longer constricted his chest.

'And the trousers and underwear,' said Zoe.

Martin sat on the plush chair, carefully unlacing and removing each glossy black Oxford shoe. In no time at all, Martin was left completely exposed and tightly fastened to the chair using the ropes from the bag. All eyes were fixed on him, making him feel self-conscious. His eyes were closed, blocking out the world around him. He felt a wave of helplessness wash over him. He did not enjoy the piercing gazes directed towards him, particularly Fedya's, with a smug smirk of derision etched on his face. Martin knew it was Fedya who had come up with the latest move in the game, as he recognized his distinct style of play. Determination filled his mind as he reminded himself, 'I must get through this.' He must help Zoe complete the task as well.

Martin's gaze fell to the floor before timidly glancing up at Zoe, dressed in a French maid costume. She looked irresistibly alluring. Her presence stirred a deep sense of desire within him. She stirred in him a mix of passionate desire and a bittersweet melancholy. He experienced a mix of sensual pleasure and bittersweet remorse for the pain he had caused her. Her essence seemed to seep into every corner of his being, leaving no room for escape. Following the card's instructions, Zoe twisted his nipples with relentless force, causing a mix of pleasure and pain to surge through him. She then leaned forward, pressing the tops of her breasts against his face. Her hair brushed against his cheek, tickling his skin as he could feel her hot breath on his face.

'Lick them!' Zoe commanded..

Martin leaned in closer, his tongue delicately tasting each breast. The aroma of her desire was unmistakable to him. In front of all the people in the audience, a small communion of passion unfolded.

Martin blushed and felt his cheeks grow warm as he hardened in front of Fedya's close friends. Helplessness washed over him like a suffocating wave.

Zoe's eyes widened as she saw Martin's bulging muscles, tightly bound to the chair, his mouth agape and his eyes filled with fear. Zoe gently caressed his cheek, feeling her heart pound in her chest. His body trembled with a mix of cold and embarrassment, making it hard for him to steady himself. The scent of bitter orange and nutmeg lingered around Martin.

'Don't worry, Martin,' she said reassuringly. She reassured herself, thinking, 'This will be over soon.'

The dancefloor was bathed in the soft notes of a sensual, slow song. Zoe danced in time to the sultry rhythm, feeling the music course through her veins.

Zoe's voice echoed through the ballroom as she boldly declared, 'David, I want you to ravish me.'

Fedya clapped, and the sound of his hands coming together echoed through the air. Then, the rest of the crowd joined in, their applause filling the room. In perfect sync with the music, Fedya clapped his hands, adding an extra layer of sound to the melody.

Zoe gently pressed her lips against the smooth lips of the statue of David. She gently kissed each nipple, leaving a cold sensation against her lips. She made a sensuous sound, reminiscent of devouring a ripe peach, as exquisitely sculpted marble shone with her saliva.

Zoe then straddled the statue, grinding her hips against the marble, feeling a mix of pleasure and humiliation.

'The bouncer and the statue are the best lovers I have ever had,' Zoe exclaimed, her voice echoing through the crowded room.

Fedya stepped forward, unzipping his fly, a mischievous glint in his eyes as he said, 'Wait darling, I have something special to share with you tonight that I think will change your mind.'

GARDEN

Zoe and Martin walked along the promenade of Jardin des Tuileries arm in arm. A light wind whistled through the trees.

'Are you OK?' asked Zoe.

'Of course. Why do you ask?'

'After last night.'

'It felt very weird being bound to the chair and feeling such desire for you and being exposed to the glare of so many people when experiencing something so intimate.'

'All I want to do is make you happy,' said Zoe.

'You do, and you do it in the strangest ways.'

'Tell me does Fedya have control over you?'

'He is connected to some powerful people. He appears to just be a hedonist pursuing his next pleasure, but he is also a hard-headed businessman. I hate to say it, but he has outplayed me in the game of business. He dangled the bait on the hook and Elke, and I took it.'

'Is he the reason you and Elke devised the game?'

There was a long pause. Another couple passed by. The woman was pregnant. Her husband had his arm around her shoulder.

'Fedya instructed us to begin the game. If Elke wins, then you must surrender to her and do as she wishes. I suspect Fedya would direct Elke to hand you over to him to join his harem in Saint Petersburg.'

'What if I refused to go?'

'Fedya would extract a price in some other way.'

'In what way?'

'I don't know, but I would not want to cross him.'

'How do we get out of this awful situation?'

'You just have to win the game.'

'In other words, we must come up with a sexual challenge that Elke cannot fulfil.'

'Yes,' said Martin.

'If Elke loses, then she will get out of our lives and let us be a couple?'

'Yes.'

'Will Fedya be out of our lives as well?'

'Yes.'

'Then tell me how to win this game.'

There was silence for a moment.

'Elke loves being free and being unconstrained by society or people's expectations. She would find being bound very difficult, as I did.'

'If we are to succeed, then that is what we must set for Elke's next challenge.'

LIBRARY

Elke entered the reading room of the Bibliotheque Nationale de France on the Rue de Richelieu, where white arches and large circular skylights filled the space with natural light. The room was bathed in a warm, golden light, illuminating the rows of leather-bound books that lined the walls, each one a treasure trove of accumulated wisdom. She had a mobile telephone earpiece tucked into her ear. Sitting in her living room, Zoe looked out at the grey clouds floating over the Paris rooftops as she spoke on the telephone.

'Proceed to the reading room and take Le Monde from the newspaper stand and sit at a desk opposite someone,' said Zoe.

Elke took the newspaper and sat across from a well-groomed man in a checkered jacket, crisp white shirt, and a blue tie. He had a sturdy build, soft brown hair, and contemplative blue eyes, giving off the impression of a businessman enjoying a peaceful moment during his lunch break in the library.

Elke's gaze met his, and he glanced up from his leather-bound book, offering her a fleeting smile. The winter sunshine streamed through the large skylights above them, casting heavenly rays onto the floor.

'Stare at the person in front of you,' said Zoe.

The man looked up and caught the woman opposite him, gazing into his eyes. She had a graceful figure, with captivating eyes that were captivatingly large. He wondered if he had seen her before somewhere - perhaps on a larger-than-life billboard or within the glossy pages of a magazine. What was her desire? A warm smile spread across his face once more.

'Lick your lips,' said Zoe.

Elke followed Zoe's direction.

'Stretch and let your hair down,' Zoe said.

Elke had captured the man's undivided attention. His eyes followed her, rising and extending towards the sky, as if trying to capture every detail. Her neck stretched, her chest pushed out, and her long hair cascaded down her shoulders like a flowing wave. Her flawless complexion radiated a natural glow, accentuated by the beautiful arch of her brows and the striking symmetry of her face.

The man stood there, unsure of his next move. All he knew was that she was giving him permission to observe her, and he couldn't tear his eyes away.

'Beckon the person to come towards you,' said Zoe.

Elke smiled warmly at the stranger and tilted her head, silently inviting him to come closer. The stranger looks over his shoulder, searching for any signs of someone else she might be gesturing to, before realizing she was pointing at him. Each nodded.

'Good day, mademoiselle. How can I help you?'

'Tell him to follow you,' said Zoe through the mouthpiece into Elke's ear.

Elke smiled at the stranger and said, 'Follow me.'

Elke glanced over her shoulder and saw the stranger trailing behind her as she approached the spiral staircase. His eyes were drawn irresistibly to Elke's enticing backside, swaying seductively before him. Elke's outfit consisted of black tights that stopped mid-thigh, paired with a mini blazer featuring pleats. He could almost see up her dress, but he knew he should not look.

'Where are we going? What do you want?' the stranger asked.

'Tell him you want to surrender to him,' said Zoe.

'I want to surrender to you,' said Elke.

'What? I don't understand,' said the stranger.

'Find an aisle with no-one in it,' said Zoe.

Elke looked down one aisle and then another. Each one had someone reading a book within it. Finally, Elke found an aisle with no one down it. Zoe's next instructions made Elke's face flush with embarrassment. Without uttering a word, Elke took off her shoes, peeled down her rights and removed her panties and handed them all over to the stranger.

'Sir, you are the sexiest man I have ever seen, and I want you to dominate me,' Elke whispered, trying not to attract the attention of the other library users.

'I don't know what to say,' the stranger said. 'You're gorgeous. What do you want me to do with these?'

'Sir, please tie my hands behind my back with my panties,' Elke said. 'Tie them tightly.'

The stranger obediently followed the instructions given to him. Elke then knelt down, using her mouth to undo the stranger's zipper and carefully removing his underwear with her teeth.

Nervously, the stranger glanced behind him, his manhood exposed. Elke's gentle licks were akin to a cat delicately lapping up cream. She then gently kissed and caressed his shaft with her lips. The stranger's touch sent a shiver down Elke's spine as his fingers found her nipples beneath the blazer, gently rolling them between his fingertips, causing them to harden. Her tongue was slick and velvety as it glided along his shaft. The stranger felt lightheaded as Elke's mouth enveloped him, while his fingers gently caressing his hair.

'Now tell him you want him to take you from behind,' said Zoe.

Moving her head away from the stranger's rigid shaft, Elke observed it quivering in the air, as if on the brink of explosion. Elke then stood up, planting her feet firmly and widening her legs.

'Sir, please hold my arms behind me and take me from behind,' said Elke.

The stranger's gaze lingered on Elke's bare buttocks, appreciating their firm and rounded shape. With two fingers, he gently parted her labia, revealing Elke's passionate core. Elke inhaled deeply, filling her lungs with the crisp, fresh air.

'Monsieur, I need you to penetrate me deeply. More deeply than any man has ever penetrated me before,' said Elke.

The tight bindings of the panties around Elke's wrists made her acutely aware of her vulnerability and helplessness. The stranger pushed deep within her, feeling the tightness of her embrace around his member.

'Is this a dream? You are incredible,' said the stranger. 'So hot.'

Elke moaned unabashedly, her sounds of pleasure filling the air without a care for anyone listening. With her mouth open in astonishment, the librarian, sporting oversized black glasses, gazed on the couple with her hands planted on her waist.

'What is going on here?'

The librarian's words came out as a harsh whisper, but the couple seemed oblivious, their only response being the sound of passionate moaning. Elke's body was consumed by intense vibrations, moaning more loudly so that everyone in the library was staring at the strange spectacle.

CHECKMATE

The room was illuminated by the late sunlight filtering in through the grand windows in Fedya's apartment. As Zoe sat on a brown chesterfield couch, she took in the spaciousness of the large living room. In front of her, there was a wooden coffee table adorned with a purple mask and a menacing black whip with a handle made of black wood. In the corner of the room, there was an object concealed under a white sheet, resembling a ghostly figure from an old film.

'It's a beautiful moon tonight, is it not?' said Fedya, approaching Zoe and stroking her cheek like she already belonged to him.

'It is,' said Zoe.

'Do you believe it makes all the gargoyles of Paris come alive?' asked Fedya.

'I don't know.'

Fedya laughed and said, 'I know that for a fact, my darling and you look exquisite in that same moonlight.'

'Thankyou.'

'I have plans for you, Zoe. There is a mask on the table in front of you. Put it on.'

Zoe's fingers delicately grasped the Venetian masquerade mask, feeling the softness of the purple sequins and the gentle tickle of the large purple feather. The mask fit perfectly, moulding to the contours of her face.

'Stand up,' commanded Fedya.

Zoe hesitated for a moment, then slowly rose from her seat. Her satin dress accentuated every contour of her figure. She was naked under the dress, as Elke instructed. Her figure was on full display in the form-fitting dress. As Fedya's fingers danced across her chest, Zoe felt a tingling sensation building within her.

'That's how your nipples will always be for me when you are my maid, Zoe,' said Fedya, chuckling to himself. 'You must always be aroused and ready for me to penetrate you. We might shop at Gostiny Dvor or walking through the Udelnaya Flea Market. You must always be wet for me. I might take you in the changing room or behind the bins in the street. Do you understand and accept this Zoe?'

Zoe stood there silently, her mind racing as she weighed the stakes of winning the game - staying with Martin in Paris or being separated, cast away with Elke in Berlin or Fedya in Russia.

'You don't answer me, but I know you. I know what you really want,' said Fedya, brushing the back of his hand along the sides of Zoe's breasts. 'Am I right?'

'Yes, sir,' said Zoe, looking forward.

'And I am the gargoyle?'

'Yes, sir.'

'The Hunchback of Notre Dame?'

'Yes, sir.'

'Quasimodo who turned to human beings with regret when he would rather be with the saints and monsters looking down from the cathedral?'

'Yes, sir,' said Zoe, not really understanding what Freya meant.

'Like Victor Hugo said - the saints are my friends and blessed me and the monsters are my friends and guard me.'

The game tonight was to comply with his wishes without question until he signalled its end. Zoe thought it wouldn't be a difficult task, but with Fedya, the game could take unexpected turns.

'I want you to listen to me and listen to me carefully. I will only tell you this once. When you are with me, there are rules and failing to obey the rules will cause severe punishment. Is that understood?'

'Yes.'

'Yes, what?'

'Yes, sir.'

'Rule number one is that my instructions must be obeyed to the letter. No ifs, or buts or maybes.'

'Yes, sir.'

'If I tell you to strip, what do you do?'

'I strip, sir.'

'If I tell you to do this in the middle of a busy street, what do you do?'

'I still strip, sir.'

'If I tell you to pleasure yourself, what do you do?'

'I pleasure myself, sir.'

'For how long?'

'Until you say stop, sir.'

'If I tell you to pleasure someone else, what do you do?'

'I pleasure them, sir.'

'And how do you pleasure them?'

'How I am instructed to pleasure them, sir.'

'If I tell you to display yourself, what do you do?'

'I display myself, sir.'

'When I get you to Russia, I want you constantly on display. When I get home from my business meetings, I want you kneeling head to the floor, bottom in the air and spreading your labia. You must always be wet and ready for me so start masturbating half an hour before I arrive home.'

'Yes, sir.'

As Fedya picked up the bulbous black whip, he could feel its weight in his hand.

'Raise your dress, my darling,' said Fedya.

Zoe bent over, lifting the hem of her dress and revealing her bare buttocks illuminated by the moonlight. Fedya runs his hand over her bottom, feeling the smoothness of her skin.

'So smooth and round,' said Fedya. 'You are a divine work of nature. You have the shapeliest ass I have ever seen.'

'Thank you, sir.'

In anticipation, Zoe felt a slight shiver run down her spine. Fedya used his knee to gently nudge her legs apart, spreading her. He traced his fingers along the crease between her legs, eliciting an involuntary moan from Zoe.

'I love your heels. You seem to have legs that go on forever,' said Fedya.

'Thank you, sir,' replied Zoe.

'I also love your labia my darling, so pink and thirsty for attention,' says Fedya. 'They speak to me.'

'Thank you, sir.'

'You know what they are saying?'

'No, sir.'

Fedya chuckles to himself then says, 'Please take me, Fedya. We are hungry for you.'

'Yes, sir,' said Zoe.

'Ride this,' said Fedya, holding the handle of the whip up to Zoe's face then positioning it between her legs. 'Rock back and forth upon it.'

Zoe slide herself over the handle of the whip and back again until it is slick from her.

'Do you like the handle of the whip, Zoe?'

'Yes, sir.'

'But you would like my penis better, is that it?' Fedya asked, laughing.

'Yes, sir. Of course.'

'Imagine my index finger is my penis. Take it in your mouth and make me climax,' said Fedya.

With anticipation, Zoe's mouth opened to take in Fedya's finger, as he expertly teased her with the handle of the whip between her legs. Zoe's slurping sounds echoed in the room as she eagerly sucked on Fedya's finger.

'I like your technique,' said Fedya. 'Twisting his finger and exploring her mouth, smearing her lipstick on her skin. 'I can see you have excellent technique. Martin has trained you very well.'

Zoe stops sucking Fedya's finger and says,' Thank you, sir.'

'Did I tell you to stop sucking?'

'No, sir. Sorry, sir.'

Zoe resumed sucking Fedya's finger eagerly, but it was too late, and Fedya's expression turned sour.

'I take that back about Martin training you well,' Fedya says harshly. 'Only speak when I want you to speak.'

'Sorry, sir,' Zoe mumbled with the finger still in her mouth.

'You did it again. How many lashes of the whip do you deserve, Zoe?'

Zoe sucked Fedya's finger with even greater force. She hoped her efforts would prevent Fedya from punishing her. Furthermore, she had received no indication to cease. Fedya withdrew his finger and also the handle of the whip.

'Now answer me,' Fedya growled.

'I don't know what to say, sir,' said Zoe before biting her bottom lip.

'Lie down over the back of the sofa with your dress raised and your legs apart,' ordered Fedya.

'Yes, sir,' said Zoe, complying with Fedya's directions.

'Hands out straight and together,' said Fedya.

Once Zoe completed her task, Fedya swiftly secured handcuffs around her wrists, the sound of the locks clicking echoing in the room. He then picked up a dining chair and positioned himself right behind Zoe, the scent of his lit cigar filling the air.

'As I said behind your behind truly is exquisite, Zoe.' said Fedya, jiggling her buttocks with his one hand while puffing on the cigar with the other. 'What do you say?'

'Thank you, sir.'

'Wiggle your bottom for me, princess,' said Fedya.

Zoe wiggled from side to side, making her bottom sway.

'You do that well. Now you didn't answer me before about how many times you should be whipped.'

'Please don't whip me, sir,' said Zoe, her voice trembling.

Fedya couldn't tear his eyes away from Zoe's perfectly shaped behind. Her skin had a subtle rosy glow, as if reflecting the soft light of a sunset.

'But how can I punish you so that you learn the importance of obedience, my darling,' said Fedya, gently stroking up and down between her legs and expertly stimulating Zoe's soft inner lips.

'I will do anything,' says Zoe breathlessly. Despite herself she could feel herself becoming wet.

'Will you devote your mouth to me?'

'Yes, sir?'

'Who does this belong to?' asked Fedya, circling Zoe's clitoris and then reaching with two fingers to her G spot and moving his finger expertly in a come-hither motion, making Zoe close her eyes to savour the moment.

'You sir,' Zoe said.

'Who will you think of when you masturbate in the shower?'

'You, sir.'

'Who will you dream about penetrating you?'

'You, sir.'

'Who will you beg to penetrate you every moment of the day?'

'You, sir.'

'Do other men mean anything to you?'

'No, sir.'

'Who are you devoted to?'

'You, sir.'

'Look behind you,' said Fedya, moving the chair and then going over to the corner of the room and removing the sheet. Martin stood there, his tall frame casting a shadow on the floor. He is tied in knots, naked and brooding, crouching on the floor, lean torso, and muscled arms. Fedya walked over to Martin and unsheathed a knife from under his jacket and cut Martin loose.

'Martin, prepare Zoe for me. I want all her entrances ready. Crawl on your hands and knees.'

Martin kept his head down and crawled on all fours towards Zoe, who was sprawled over the back of the couch. He knelt down and carefully pushed Zoe's dress further up, placing his head between her legs and exploring her centre with his tongue.

'Very good Martin. Lick slowly. We have all night,' said Fedya who walked towards Zoe so that his crotch was next to her face and unzipped his trousers, releasing his large member. He then pulled Zoe forward by her arms and held her aloft as she took his member in her mouth and sucked it.

Zoe let out a soft whimper, her body trembling as Martin's gentle touch explored every curve and crevice, his tongue slowly gliding between her legs. She pressed into him, absorbing the comfort of his undivided attention.

'Martin, now lie down on the floor.'

Once Martin is lying down, Fedya says, 'Now Zoe get up off the couch and sit on Martin's face.'

Zoe's hands tightly clasped in front of her, her dress cascading around Martin's head as she squatted down, her stilettos wobbling beneath her with each movement, intensifying the sensation as she felt his tongue exploring her, delving even deeper than before.

Fedya did his trousers up and sat on the chesterfield and took sips of whisky from his glass as he watches the spectacle. As Fedya placed the glass back on the coffee table, Zoe's ears caught the delicate sound of ice clinking within. Her senses came alive as she was surrounded by an overwhelming array of sensations.

'OK that's enough of that. Stand up Zoe.'

'Yes, sir.'

'Let me look at you. Come here.'

Zoe tottered over on her stilettos, her steps unsteady and her hands still bound by the handcuffs. As she stood in front of him, she could feel the intensity of his gaze. Remaining seated on the couch, he gently lifted her dress and inhaled her intoxicating scent.

Fedya whispered, 'The scent of a woman's arousal is intoxicating,' as he leaned in close, inhaling deeply. Zoe felt like she might topple over and fall on him.

'Would you like Martin to penetrate you now? To drive you into another dimension of pleasure?'

'Yes, sir.'

'I knew that would be your answer somehow. You are so ripe and luscious like a ripe peach waiting to be devoured,' said Fedya, unzipping his trousers and pulling out his penis.

'You may have your Martin, but you will continue to pleasure me with your mouth at the same time.'

Zoe bent over. It was hard for her to reach his penis with her mouth. Perched high above him, she struggled to maintain her balance with her hands tightly clasped together. Her tongue stretched out as she licked the tip of Fedya's penis, her hands pressed together on the couch beside him.

'If you fall, my dear, there will be consequences for both you and for Martin. Very severe consequences,' said Fedya menacingly. 'Martin, you know what to do.'

Zoe persistently attempted to reach Fedya's penis with her tongue and mouth, but only managed to brush against the tip. This was the moment of truth, she thought, as her heart raced with anticipation. You must endure and overcome this challenging trial. She tried to take more of his member into her mouth, feeling the softness of his skin against her lips, while Martin's hands moved up her thighs, lifting her cocktail dress and entering her with a tender touch. His hands on her hips grounded her, providing a sense of stability as Fedya's arousal intensified, heightening her ability to connect with him.

Martin rocked into her, and she could feel his presence filling her completely, their movements synchronised with a steady rhythm.

'You really are a natural at this, Zoe. You are too beautiful to be limited to one man. I have parties in Russia. You will make love to a hundred men in one night and love it.'

Fedya's comment fueled Zoe's determination to conquer the challenge and emerge victorious from this maddening game. With her last ounce of strength, she engulfed Fedya's arousal with her mouth. He was now as hard as stone, his body quivering with anticipation. Without a doubt, he was eager to come, and the challenge would soon reach its conclusion. Fedya tossed his head back, a mischievous glint in his eyes.

'That feels amazing my darling. Martin be a good man and pick up the pace. No slacking off. I want Zoe to come as I shoot my load into her throat.'

Zoe tried to focus on the job at hand, but Martin's slow and steady thrusts are causing her to lose focus as overlapping sensations rippled within her that felt like they are culminating into a fire that would consume her and she made little animalistic grunts when she took breaths between sucking Fedya who was now roughly handling her voluptuous breasts then cruelly squeezing her nipples and twisting them. She found Fedya's cruel treatment of her both repulsive and strangely thrilling. Lower and lower she pressed her mouth and throat onto him. Her ruby red lips could almost reach the base of his erection as the tip glanced across the skin of her throat. She felt Fedya's hot breath upon her and his heart beating fast.

'Faster Martin,' urged Fedya like he is a jockey riding a horse in a horse race.

Zoe's knees trembled with pleasure as Martin thrust passionately from behind, sending waves of ecstasy coursing through her body. She crumbled to the floor in an awkward heap, her forehead accidentally colliding with Fedya's midsection, eliciting a sharp cry of pain.

Zoe was shocked beyond words, struggling to accept that this had really happened. Her gaze remained fixated on the floor, unable to lift her eyes.

'You silly girl. What have you done?' yelled Fedya.

'I'm sorry, sir,' said Zoe meekly on the floor.

'Look at me when you talk to me,' said Fedya.

Zoe looked up at Fedya, her eyes misting with tears.

'You silly young woman,' said Fedya.

'I'm so very sorry, sir. I didn't mean to do that. I lost my balance.'

'Martin rip her dress off,' commanded Fedya.

Martin looked at Zoe collapsed on the floor and felt tremendous regret at getting her involved in all of this. This was all his fault.

'No, I will not do that, Fedya,' said Martin.

'Are you disobeying me, Martin?'

'Yes, I am.'

'Do you hear that, Zoe? What happens when people disobey me, Zoe?'

Zoe looked up at Fedya, sitting on the couch. He was like Jeckle and Hyde, turning from a regular man into a monster.

'What happens to people who disobey me, Zoe?' Fedya asked even louder.

'They are punished,' Zoe said quietly, almost inaudibly.

'Martin, lie down on the floor.'

Martin looked at Zoe then at Fedya.

'This is your last chance, Martin. If you fail in this task, then I win the game and Zoe will belong to Elke and to me.'

Martin lay down on the wooden floor. He was still half erect.

'That's right Martin, now put your hands out flat on the floor,' says Fedya.

'Now Zoe you stand up.'

Zoe awkwardly got up from the ground and looked down on Martin who had closed his eyes.

'OK Zoe. Kick Martin in the crotch. Do it with all your might.'

'No, I couldn't possibly do that. I would hurt him.'

'Do it now, my darling, or you lose the game.'

Zoe looked to Martin who opened his eyes and says, 'It's OK Zoe, do it. I will be fine. Let's finish this.'

Zoe delicately lifted her foot, tapping it softly between his legs.

Fedya laughed. 'That was not a kick. That was a love tap. Now stand on his hands.'

'I can't do that I could break the bones in his hands,' said Zoe pleadingly.

'Do it Zoe. I'll be fine,' said Martin.

Zoe walked towards Martin and stood astride his naked body and lifted one foot over Martin's hand, but then she removed it again.

'I can't do it,' said Zoe with an exasperated sigh.

'What's that?'

'I can't do it, sir.'

'You understand what this means don't you?'

'Yes, I do.'

'You have now lost the game,' said Fedya with a cruel smile on his lips.

ISLAND

Zoe stood on the Pont Neuf bridge, taking in the panoramic view of the Seine as it flowed beneath her. It touched down on Île de la Cité, the island in the middle of Paris that was filled with the echoes of centuries past. The remnants of the ancient city of Lutetia can still be seen, a haunting reminder of the past. Above the traffic noise, a male busker with a twirly handlebar moustache sang 'La Mer' in a deep, resonant baritone.

'What are we going to do, Martin?' Zoe said, as a barge passed under the bridge. "I can't leave you or Paris. What about my studies?'

'I'm sorry but we knew the rules of the game,' said Martin.

'Can't we just escape somewhere? Change our identities?' asked Zoe.

'Elke is working for Fedya. He has eyes everywhere. You know his nickname is the Wolf. He is very powerful, with ties right up to the top of the Russian elites. There is no point running from them.'

'Can we continue the game or ask for another game?'

Martin did not say anything.

'Is there nothing we can do?'

'I feel like you are a part of me. I feel like I am being separated from part of myself. The part of me that is wild and passionate. The part of me that feels love. The part of me which is alive,' says Martin.

'Let's go somewhere together. Somewhere Fedya would not find us. Just you and I.'

'There is no such place. You don't break contracts with Fedya. He is charming when he wants something from you but lethal if you cross him.'

'What does Fedya have over you?'

'I'm heavily indebted to him. I have to admit that the game was his idea. If I disappeared with you, then he would be furious and have us tracked down. He has connections with the secret service. It wouldn't be hard for him to find us. Also, without his influence and money my businesses would be finished. I am now powerless against his wishes. I'm just an empty vessel being blown along by the wind.'

'So this is where our story ends?' Zoe felt a tear travel down her cheek. 'Am I so disposable to you?'

'No, absolutely not. You are the most precious thing in my life,' Martin's eyes are wet as well. 'The only way I can protect you is to have you agree to the wishes of Elke and Fedya. The thing is we would both be in danger if we breached an agreement. As I said, Fedya is merciless with people who breach agreements. He goes to any length to get what he wants.'

'You would have me live with and submit to people so dangerous?'

'You must be careful of who you make enemies of. You want dangerous people to be close to you - to be your defender instead of your aggressor. The only way for us both to be safe is to follow through on the rules of the game and for you to go with Elke as her prize. Elke has directed that you go to Russia with Fedya.'

'But what is my life going to be like after today?'

'You will have a life of exceptional luxury. Fedya will put millions in your bank account. You will want for nothing. The best food. Expensive fashion. Travel.'

'It will all be meaningless if I don't have you beside me,' said Zoe. 'Also, what about my studies? What will I tell my professor?'

'You are very intelligent. You will think of something. Also, once you are on the inside of their lives, you will find a way to freedom. You will find a way back to me and Paris. I will always be at the end of your phone. You will not be alone. I will be with you the whole time in spirit.'

'I don't know if I can stand not being able to touch you. To feel the warmth of your body next to mine. I only agreed to this stupid game so we could be together, and you would be exclusive to me and we could be a family together.'

'We are still a family, and we will be together I promise you. I trust you to find a way back to me. Fedya loves games, and he stands by his agreements. You will find your way through the puzzle and return to Paris. This time with Elke and Fedya will pass and then we will be together and safe,' said Martin, wrapping his arm around Zoe's shoulder.

They embraced each other and become one with their arms wrapped around each other as the dark suited stream of pedestrians passed on either side of them like they were an island in the river.

Thank you for reading this erotica novel.
We hope you enjoyed it and welcome your feedback.
Please leave an honest review where you purchased this novel or
provide feedback on our website[1] through the feedback form.

---

1. https://minuetpublishing.wixsite.com/books

Nicolas Blanc
FRENCH
MAID

FRENCH MAID[1]
BELLE FLEUR EROTICA
VOLUME 1

Zoe Fabrice, a young and beautiful Parisian university student obtains a vacation job as a maid at the chateau of the mysterious Martin Dore. Zoe's attraction to her boss draws her into increasingly more decadent and dangerous sexual escapades as Martin and his friend Elke test Zoe's boundaries. Zoe wants to find out if eroticism can translate into something more with Martin but is Elke helping or hindering this quest?

French Maid is the first book in the Belle Fleur Erotica Series and is a sizzling and sexy read for lovers of classic erotica in the style of Emmanuelle and Fifty Shades of Grey.

---

1. https://books2read.com/b/frenchmaid

NICOLAS BLANC
MAID FOR
PLEASURE

MAID FOR PLEASURE[1]
BELLE FLEUR EROTICA
VOLUME 3

Having lost the game in House of Games, Zoë must submit to Elke and leave Martin and Paris behind. Will Zoë be able to escape the depravity of St Petersburg and return to Martin in Paris or will she be condemned to serve Fedya and satiate his bizarre sexual perversions forever?

---

1. https://minuetpublishing.wixsite.com/books

EROTICA
Nicolas Blanc
THE PLEASURE OF SURRENDER
BOOK ONE IN THE "EROTICA" SERIES
Nicolas Blanc
EROTICA 2
SECRETARY
Nicolas Blanc
EROTICA 3
EMPIRE

2

THE EROTICA COLLECTION[1]

The *Erotica Collection*[2] features *Erotica: The Pleasure of Surrender*, *Secretary* and *Empire*.

In *Erotica: The Pleasure of Surrender*[3], Aaron and Candice, a married couple separately become the pawns of Olivia, a beautiful and powerful businesswoman, who revels in the control and manipulation of others for her own selfish amusement. Both Aaron and Candice are drawn into increasingly bizarre sexual adventures at the instigation of Olivia, neither of them aware that she is also doing the same with their spouse.

In *Secretary*[4], Jillian is a beautiful secretary in the thrall of her powerful and domineering boss, Olivia, and will do anything she can to please Olivia's dark erotic desires in the bedroom, in the office and at Olivia's country mansion where Jillian must fulfil the sexual demands of a secret society of rich businesswomen.

In *Empire*[5], Olivia Harrison seeks revenge against Antoinette Ward, her arch business rival, moving her pawns against those closest to her rival - Antoinette's partner, Tina Scott, Antoinette's conservative brother and sister in law, Toby and Brook Ward, and Dean Bailey, Antoinette's business mentor. Antoinette finds out what Olivia is up to and joins the dangerous chess game of sexual intrigue, seduction, and power with each woman wanting to prevail and build their Empire.

---

1. https://books2read.com/eroticacollection

2. *https://books2read.com/eroticacollection*

3. *https://books2read.com/erotica*

4. *https://books2read.com/secretary*

5. *https://books2read.com/empire*

PARANORMAL ROMANCE
NICOLAS BLANC
THE
DARK
MERMAID
SIREN'S SONG

NICOLAS BLANC
THE DARK MERMAID[1]

In *The Dark Mermaid: Siren's Song*, Madelaine travels to a remote Thai island which is promised to be incredibly beautiful and uninhabited, to renew herself after the end of a disastrous relationship. Madelaine's fellow backpackers on the island, Marco, Matias, Arvid, and Eugenie are also seeking renewal after difficult times in Europe. The island is beautiful as promised but not uninhabited and the backpackers must engage in an epic struggle with the inhabitants of the island.

In the course of their struggle, Madelaine starts to develop a relationship with one of the other backpackers but finds that she has a love rival from the island, The Dark Mermaid.

---

1. https://books2read.com/mermaid

Edited by Claire Quinn
SCIENCE FICTION
EROTICA 1
Mars and Venus

SCIENCE FICTION EROTICA 1[1]

OK now think of your wildest sexual fantasy...one that rocks your intergalactic spaceship ... OK? Now multiply the kinkiness factor in your fantasy by warp speed ... got that? OK now you're accelerating through space and your mind and your body are tingling. Hmm...now you have an idea of where *Science Fiction Erotica 1: Mars and Venus is* coming from. Let your fantasies get away with themselves in every wicked way possible. Science Fiction Erotica 1: Mars and Venus is a highly charged erotic mix of short stories featuring libidinous sex bots, abductions by hunky aliens, mad mind controlling scientists, frisky new world colonists, and tentacle monsters. Enjoy.

---

1. https://books2read.com/sciencefiction

THE SCIENCE FICTION AND FANTASY EROTICA COLLECTION[1]

Minuet Publishing has collected together for you three steamy books of science fiction and fantasy erotica.

Book 1 is the *Science Fiction Erotica Collection* - a selection of sizzling science fiction short stories where the imagination knows no limits.

Book 2 is Kumi Ito's *Insatiable Sex Cyborg*. When Hiroko meets Akemi she feels like she has met the man of her dreams. But Hiroko has a secret. She is a cyborg with an insatiable sex drive and is on the run from her boss, the yakuza and the Cyborg Repossession Squad. Can Akemi escape the perverted sexual demands of those who want to control her and find true love?

---

1. https://books2read.com/sfferotica

Book 3 is Nicolas Blanc's *The Dark Mermaid*.

In *The Dark Mermaid: Siren's Song*, Madelaine travels to a remote Thai island which is promised to be incredibly beautiful and uninhabited, to renew herself after the end of a disastrous relationship. Madelaine's fellow backpackers on the island, Marco, Matias, Arvid, and Eugenie are also seeking renewal after difficult times in Europe. The island is beautiful as promised but not uninhabited and the backpackers must engage in an epic struggle with the inhabitants of the island. In the course of their struggle, Madelaine starts to develop a relationship with one of the other backpackers but finds that she has a love rival from the island, *The Dark Mermaid*.

INSATIABLE
KUMI ITO

INSATIABLE[1]
BY KUMI ITO

When Hiroko meets Akemi she feels like she has met the man of her dreams. But Hiroko has a secret. She is a cyborg with an insatiable sex drive and is on the run from her boss, the yakuza and the Cyborg Repossession Squad. Can Akemi escape the perverted sexual demands of those who want to control her and find true love?

---

1. https://www.amazon.com.au/Insatiable-Sex-Cyborg-Kumi-Ito/dp/1717956645

Minuet Publishing[2]

[3]

2. https://minuetpublishing.wixsite.com/books

3. https://minuetpublishing.wixsite.com/books

Don't miss out!

Visit the website below and you can sign up to receive emails whenever Nicolas Blanc publishes a new book. There's no charge and no obligation.

https://books2read.com/r/B-A-IHVC-TOEXB

BOOKS2READ

Connecting independent readers to independent writers.